No Time to Bury Them

ALSO BY MARK C. EDDY

The Recent History of Terrorism in Canada, 1963–2013 (2014)

No Time to Bury Them

Mark C. Eddy

IGUANA

Copyright © 2017 Mark C. Eddy
Published by Iguana Books
720 Bathurst Street, Suite 303
Toronto, Ontario, Canada
M5S 2R4

Publisher: Mary Ann J. Blair
Editor: Jen R. Albert
Cover design and illustration: Mary Beth MacLean

Library and Archives Canada Cataloguing in Publication

Eddy, Mark C., 1978-, author
        No time to bury them / Mark C. Eddy.

Issued in print and electronic formats.

ISBN 978-1-77180-222-2 (softcover)
ISBN 978-1-77180-223-9 (EPUB)
ISBN 978-1-77180-224-6 (Kindle)

        I. Title.

PS8609.D49N6 2017   C813'.6   C2017-904661-6
                                        C2017-904662-4

This is an original print edition of *No Time to Bury Them*.

This book is dedicated to my brother, Robert, who always set a high standard for his siblings to reach.

Prologue

How much farther could he go? Azarov's breathing came in great movements now. Gluts of freezing air struck his lungs, giving a strange relief. Sweat ran down his body. He knew that it would later chill under his fur clothes. Maybe it would even mean his death on this trail.

The sky's fading light intensified his desperation. If Azarov didn't kill the man ahead of him, the last two days of travel would be for nothing. And how would he then answer to Morgan? What excuse could he give that would possibly satisfy his boss?

His prey lay only one hundred yards ahead of him, one hundred and thirty at the most. Even in the dying light, Azarov could see the man racing through the leafless bushes that sprouted from the snowfield like hair on the back of a frozen giant.

The man's sled dogs were unexhausted. Their barks and yelps hadn't ceased. Azarov's own dogs, now halted, lay panting in the snow. Behind him, his men watched. Their sled dogs were in equally bad condition, but no one moved to tend to them. Nor did any of them speak. They knew better than to interrupt Azarov's thoughts. Still, he could feel their worries pressing at his back, buffeting him like the high winds that had helped to push them along the trail these last few hours.

Azarov snapped his rifle to his shoulder. He adjusted the rear sight and took the last moment to catch his breath. Across the snowfield, his prey widened the distance between them. The shot became more difficult with each passing second.

He squeezed the trigger. The rifle's crack sounded throughout the wilderness. His target spun and fell onto the front of his dogsled. Azarov had hoped he would fall to its side, into the snow. But the sled continued onwards, carrying its owner through the Yukon wilderness.

Azarov watched from the side of his own dogsled. He prayed he had killed the man, but he had a hunch he wasn't so lucky. His prey had escaped. There was nothing left for Azarov to do but turn and give orders to his men. He knew what needed to be done, and he already had an idea of where to do it. It was time to prepare for the coming storm.

Chapter 1

Suppertime is the best part of the day. Not the morning, when the last sensations of a warm bed are savoured. Not the end of the day, when that same warm bed awaits a worn body. No, Richard reflected, suppertime is most certainly the best part of each day. There is nothing better than stepping in from the cold, feeling that first wave of heat embrace the face, and catching the whiff of a meal through frozen nose hairs. Today, that meal would be a plate of steaming moose meat and roasted potatoes. He waited for the inn's waitress to serve it to him, and occupied himself by studying the otherwise empty dining room.

The Brownstone Inn was the closest thing to a real restaurant in Fort MacCammon, and it was more than satisfactory. A mammoth fireplace on the ground floor offered plenty of coziness. The heavy maple wood furniture provided its own warmth, the kind that only rich hardwood can give. Despite the hotel's name, the exterior of the building was made entirely of wood. From what Richard could tell, there wasn't a brown stone in the damn place.

The food was surprisingly good. Richard had once heard that the hotel's cook, Jean-Paul, was one of the best chefs back in Quebec City (and Richard figured that a person couldn't get a bad meal in that town). Why Jean-Paul would move to the Yukon was anyone's guess, but, in Richard's experience, people moved here either for work or because they were running from something. There were plenty of restaurants hiring between here and Quebec, so he concluded Jean-Paul must be running.

Richard scratched his moustache and looked through the blurred windowpane. The outside was even more lifeless than inside the Brownstone. The cold had forced the fort's residents to retreat into their homes. Except for a lone watchman making his rounds, no one was in sight.

He examined the collection of buildings huddled around the rectangular parade ground. Wooden walkways connected the buildings, which included a Mounties' barracks, an infirmary, a storehouse, and an office with a telegraph. The pong of wood smoke wafted throughout the fort, even into the Brownstone. Richard knew that it would taint his meal with an acrid taste.

The fort was never what people expected it to be. It had no watchtower or stockade, no cannons or front gate. What need was there for such defences when there were favourable relations between settlers and the original people of this land? If not for the forty-foot flagpole and the fort's sign, one might think it wasn't a fort at all.

Richard's eyes switched over to the fort's entrance. In the dim light, he could still see the sign, FORT MACCAMMON, and in smaller writing under it, ROYAL NORTH WEST MOUNTED POLICE.

Those words made him reflect on how the fort had grown over time. The fort sat on the bank of one of the Yukon's lesser-known waterways — the Little Fox River. It was built in the 1840s by the Hudson's Bay Company as a trading post. Situated high on a riverbank, the fort commanded a view of the surrounding forest, with its superabundance of wood. Access to fresh water was never a problem, and river travel made life easier in the warmer months.

Whatever the fort may have looked like sixty years ago, Richard was certain the 1907 version was far different. Fort MacCammon had grown from a trading post to a police detachment. With a small village now expanding against the fort's east side, some even called it a frontier town.

While the region's population may have fallen in recent years, Fort MacCammon had blossomed beyond anyone's expectations. The residents gossiped about the forthcoming arrival of electricity. But Richard believed that was still a long time away. It was enough of a surprise when, in 1902, missionaries had added a church there.

"Here's supper! I hope you're hungry, Inspector," Melissa, the waitress, said as she placed a plate before him.

"Thank you," he said without looking at her.

"Did you need anything else?" she said.

"I'll tell you if I need anything."

He knew she never deserved his rudeness, but he couldn't help himself. Melissa was a sweet woman, and one of her plump hands carried a bowl of chicken soup, the kind she knew he liked.

"Jean-Paul made extra, so I thought you might like some."

"Thank you so much," he replied and forced himself to smile. He was embarrassed by his impoliteness but thought it hardly mattered. It wasn't as if anyone were around to see him make an ass out of himself. His table was the only one occupied.

He cut himself a hunk of moose and swallowed after only one chew. Another hunk followed. The sky was darkening, and he felt it would soon be time to turn in. Tomorrow would be a busy day, with a Winter Patrol to take place in a couple of weeks.

Each winter, the Mounties undertook the Winter Patrol. It was a trek by dogsled from Fort MacCammon southwards to Dawson City. Along roughly forty miles of trail, the Mounties stopped at a couple of communities and work camps. The patrol normally took a few days, or a little more if the weather was disagreeable — certainly no more than five days, unless disaster struck. This was normally the time for people to lodge complaints and share concerns with the Mounties. There was also the monotony of keeping census records and tracking animal migration patterns. Richard sighed when he thought of the paperwork. Of all his duties, Richard hated the Winter

Patrol most. Or, more precisely, he hated being out there on the damn trail.

Despite its hardships, the patrol wasn't all misery, however. The patrollers were also tasked with delivering hundreds of pounds of mail along the route. This ensured their arrival was always welcome. They could count on hot meals and soft beds wherever they went.

His thoughts were interrupted when Melissa stepped over to his table. This time, he was sure to smile. "How's the food?" Melissa said.

"The food is wonderful. Still, I wouldn't mind some fresh fruit up here every now and then."

"One of the things that you miss about Toronto?"

Richard laughed. "On some days, what I wouldn't give to walk down a paved street with an orange in my hand."

Melissa laughed with him, but their moment was cut short. Richard's eyes darted to the front door when he heard rapid footsteps crunching towards it. He held his breath. Something momentous was happening. He knew whoever was about to enter the inn was coming for him. Who else was in the Brownstone to warrant the urgency?

The inn's front door flew open. It struck the wall of the porch, and Melissa stepped away from Richard's table. Without noticing what he was doing, Richard moved to his gun holster.

A moment later, a young Mountie stepped into the dining area.

"Inspector, we have a problem, sir." Richard opened his mouth to answer, but the Mountie interrupted. "A man just came into the fort, and he's been shot."

"Is he alive, Francis?" Richard asked.

"Just barely. That is, I mean, he was when I left him — "

"Let's go," Richard said. He grabbed his service cap from the table and headed for the door. He marched past Melissa without any acknowledgement. She knew not to speak then.

***

The two Mounties hurried across the parade ground towards the infirmary. Upon entering, they saw a man lying on the room's single bunk. His breathing was calm, though his abdomen was a shiny mess. The infirmary's nurse, Catherine, stood over him. Blood covered her hands up to the wrists.

She had removed the man's footwear and socks. Three of the toes on his left foot and two on the right had blackened. Richard didn't need Catherine to tell him it was severe frostbite. And he knew what treatment would follow.

The injured man squeezed his eyes shut and let tears run down his cheeks. They were probably the warmest things the unfortunate man had felt in days.

Richard turned to Francis. "Stay by the door and let no one enter, Constable."

"Yes, sir," Francis said.

Richard knelt next to the wounded man and took one of the man's soft hands in his. It was filthy from being in the woods, but it was not the hand of a working man. Richard guessed that the man was a clerk or some other type of office worker who had never built a callous in his life. He also saw the wedding band on the man's hand, and he knew that a widow was about to be made. In his other hand, the man held a crucifix that was modest, but beautifully crafted.

"The hole runs straight through his back. He's lost too much blood," Catherine said.

The hole was only as wide as a dime, but the blood pouring from it was a very deep red, almost black. It was the kind of blood that comes from deep in the body. Richard wasn't a nurse, but he didn't have to be to know the man was dying. During the war in the south of Africa, he had seen lesser wounds kill.

"It's a gunshot wound, no doubt," he said.

Catherine never questioned his expertise on such a topic.

"A hunting accident, maybe?" she said. "I don't know him, so perhaps he's another trophy hunter from America."

"No, his clothes are too well-worn." Richard said. "He's been living in the north for some time."

"So, if he isn't an American trying to bag a polar bear, then what is he?"

"Perhaps we should begin by asking who he is."

Richard leaned close to the stranger's face and spoke. "Can you hear me? What's your name?"

The man's eyes were glazed over. The pain and blood loss were too much for him. If answers were to come from this man, they had to come quickly.

"Hey, look at me. You're safe now. You are going to be fine," Richard lied. "What is your name?"

The man struggled to catch his breath. "My name is Reverend William Corbett," he said. His face twisted into a mask of pain. Richard thought he wouldn't continue, but then the reverend added, "I'm the head of St. Andrew's Anglican Church in Dawson," the man said.

Richard straightened his back. The man's neatly barbered hair and ornamental crucifix made sense now.

"Where did you come from, Reverend? From down south? Dawson?"

"Yes, Dawson City," he groaned.

"Did you do this to yourself?"

"No, he shot me on the trail. I almost made it to here. I almost — "

Who in God's name would shoot a reverend?" Catherine asked.

Richard glared at her. "Your commentary isn't required here, nurse, only your skills, thank you."

He turned back to the reverend.

"Who shot you?" Richard asked.

For the first time since Richard arrived, the reverend looked him in the eye. "Azarov," he said, as if he thought Richard would recognize the name. He did.

"Vadim Azarov. I met him years ago."

"But don't mind him shooting me. I travelled here to warn you about what's happening down in Dawson."

"Did someone there hurt someone else?" Richard said.

"Lots of people there are hurting lots of other people. It's Morgan that I've come about."

"Who's Morgan?"

The man made a low moan. "You mean you know Azarov, but you don't know his boss?" His eyes brightened with new life. "Oh, I see. The sly devils in Dawson did such a good job of keeping their business quiet that you know nothing about it."

"What are you on about, man? Quickly, we don't have any time to spare," Richard said.

He looked to Catherine for confirmation, and she nodded. This patient was fading.

"If you have a story to tell, out with it," Richard said.

Richard began to think it was too late. Then, Corbett opened his mouth.

"Eric Morgan has a gang in Dawson. The only gang in Dawson now. Over the last few years, he has become so strong that he practically runs the town. He has his filthy hand in everything — gambling, drinking, wh—

"He stopped himself and turned his eyes towards Catherine.

"Well, you know, Inspector."

"So, what of it? The mounted police in Dawson regulate all of those things. As long as the card games are fair and the prostitutes aren't robbing their customers, then it is all just honest deviance."

"That's just it. Nothing is honest about any of it! The games are all rigged. The women rob the men while they're asleep."

"Those are risks that folks take when they choose to live lives like that. I'll look into the matter, after I've tracked down Azarov for what he did to you. But to be honest, I can't say I feel too much sympathy for Morgan's customers."

Corbett's face strained. At first Richard thought it was pain, but then he realized it was exasperation.

"But that's just the start of it, Inspector. Morgan has proper-looking businesses running too. A hardware store, a dry goods store, hell, he even supplies beef to Dawson. He uses his gang to beat and scare the competition out of town. No other entrepreneur has a hope of winning a business contract with his gang around. Most are too afraid of him and he has paid off the ones who could be bought. I saw good men, strong men, men I thought would make a difference, end up among Morgan's cronies. Those who I thought would save the town became part of its scourge. Then there are the missing."

"The missing?"

"There were three citizens who spoke against Morgan. No one has seen them since May. Search parties were sent out, but not a trace was found."

Richard stared blankly. His mind wheeled over what he had just heard. Three people missing. Dawson wasn't a small town, and people occasionally went missing there, but three?

"Three missing," Richard said "There must be — "

"No mistake, Inspector. The reason why this is all news to your ears is because many of the local police detachment are paid by Morgan too."

Richard stared at the man for several seconds before speaking. What the reverend said was starting to make sense. In Richard's experience, the only time people went missing without a single clue as to what happened was when someone covered their tracks.

"Let's say that the missing people were murdered by Morgan. That still doesn't mean that Mounties are on his payroll."

"Stop, Inspector. Stop trying to shield your ears from the truth. I know how proud you Mounties are of your beloved service, but if what I'm saying is false, then how do you explain me? Why am I here bleeding to death in front of your eyes?"

Richard had no answer to that. It was just another puzzle piece for him to find. That members of the Mounted

Police would be on the payroll of a villain was unthinkable. If true, it would be the greatest corruption to ever infect the service in the Yukon.

"If what you say is true, why travel three days from Dawson to here? Why not just telegraph the news?

"I never knew it would reach the right ears ... honest ears."

Richard hadn't thought of that. If Morgan could bribe Mounties in Dawson, could he also bribe Mounties in Fort MacCammon? The sort of people who could serve as Morgan's eyes and ears? The sort of people who could block or alter messages sent between the two detachments. He would then control the flow of information on both ends. After all, it was what Richard would have done in Morgan's position. Richard rolled this over in his mind. The possibility of the man's words being truth seemed more likely.

"How long has this Morgan character been running Dawson?"

"Since the Gold Rush. I've watched that leech drain Dawson and its people for years now. By now, he has his hand in everything. From theft and arson, to extortion and murder. And now, he is about to commit his biggest theft of all."

Corbett caught a needed breath before continuing, and again Richard wondered if he would get the full story before the reverend passed. He saw that even Catherine had tilted her head in closer to hear his next words.

"There is $500,000 worth of gold sitting in a Dawson bank, the Royal Bank of Exchange. It's just waiting to get robbed one day. Morgan's friends at the police detachment have convinced the bank to transfer the gold from the bank to the Mountie detachment for their own safekeeping. On December sixteenth, Mounties are going to escort a wagon of gold from the bank to the headquarters. They won't make it. They are going to get robbed on the way."

"December sixteenth? That's only a week from now," Catherine said.

Richard shot her a look, surprised that she was paying attention to the conversation while treating her patient. "By who? Who's going to rob the Mounties?" Richard said.

"By other Mounties! They are going to pose as bandits."

"This is starting to sound too incredible to believe," Richard said to Catherine, not sure if he was trying to convince her or himself.

"Mounties heisting gold? Why, even if they did steal it, there's no way to hide half a million in stolen gold in a town the size of Dawson. It's too small a town. Someone will see something. Someone will talk."

"That's just it. The gold isn't going to be kept in Dawson. The gold will be dumped into an abandoned mine a couple of hours outside of Dawson. The dirty Mounties have already designated it as a restricted site, due to safety reasons. They told the citizens that the mine could cave in, that the shafts were flooded, and a load of other nonsense. If anyone sees the Mounties poking around there, the Mounties can just say that they were reinspecting the site."

Catherine leaned between the two men and gave the reverend some water. He nodded his gratitude.

"In the summer, when the ice thaws, they'll bring the gold back to Dawson and load it onto a freighter," the reverend continued. "It will be smuggled out as shipped mail, down the Yukon River and then to Seattle."

"After the attention from the robbery has died off," Richard said.

"Exactly."

"What then?"

"Morgan has a man in San Francisco who will exchange it for paper currency. So after this man takes his share, he'll send the remainder back to Dawson by postal service."

Richard thought about all those brown parcels of money thrown through some post office. The mail workers would never know they were delivering a king's ransom to the thieving scoundrels.

Richard tapped his fingers against his knee. It was a good plan, he thought. No one would get hurt. Ottawa and the Royal North West Mounted Police would never suspect its own members were culprits. By the time anyone outside of Dawson criticized the investigation, the gold would have already been converted and the money mailed to the north.

"You know this Morgan character's plans and operations in great detail, Reverend Corbett. Why?"

"Why do you think, Inspector? People confide in the clergymen, including some of Morgan's accomplices." The reverend winced, caught his breath, and gasped. His speech had sounded normal up to this point. Richard could have forgotten the man had a hole blown through him.

"We need to catch Morgan now, before he slips away. He intends to quit the Yukon and move to America come summertime, Inspector."

"He has it all figured out, doesn't he? If this has been going on for years, why didn't you come forward before now, Reverend?"

"For so long, I told myself that if I betrayed the confidence of those who had confided in me, I would be endangering their lives. I hoped that the situation would be remedied by The Almighty. I thought that God would deliver his own justice in his own time," the reverend finished.

Richard rolled his eyes at that. "And he would clean Dawson of all the sinners, Reverend?"

"Are you religious, Inspector?"

"I believe in God, if that's what you mean. But I have been away from him for a while."

Richard shifted in his seat slightly, but forced himself to stop. He hated feeling like a squirming schoolboy being questioned by his teacher, and talking about his relationship with The Almighty was uncomfortable under the best of circumstances.

"Enough about me and him. What you've told me is enough for me to apprehend Azarov and to travel to Dawson to investigate, but I don't have any hard evidence against Morgan."

"I've given my account, witnessed by them," Corbett said and nodded to Catherine and Francis.

"Do you think that I can get it in writing? That is, I can write it for you, and you only have to verify the truth of my writing and sign it."

"Yes, but I have something else that may be far more useful. Morgan killed two of his own men: Roy Alderman and his brother Lawrence Alderman. Both of them witnessed Morgan kill two of the townspeople who went missing. They panicked. Talked about travelling up to the Northwest Territories, to Fort McPherson, and reporting it to the Mounties there. The Alderman boys figured the police in Fort McPherson were beyond Morgan's reach. They had come to me before, but this time, the two brothers wanted me to help them write confession letters that they could hand over to the police. Both men were illiterate, and they wanted letters that made them sound as free of responsibility as possible. So, I agreed.

Morgan must have gotten wind of their plans; the two brothers went missing on the same day. For me, that was the breaking point. I went to their homes and searched for the letters that we had prepared together. I thought maybe Morgan never knew that they had been written. I tore their homes apart looking for them, and God was on my side."

The reverend pointed to the table next to the bed. Two letters lay there. Smears of his blood covered their envelopes.

"Those are signed letters, detailing the murders and Morgan's other crimes."

Richard's heart stopped beating. If what the reverend said was true, if there was a crime lord in Dawson and these were signed, first-hand accounts from his accomplices, then this could be the easiest big catch of any Mountie in the history of the Mounted Police.

For the next twenty minutes, Richard scribbled out Corbett's story in his notebook while Catherine battled to control the bleeding from Corbett's wound. Francis watched from his post at the doorway, quiet. When Richard finished, the reverend signed and dated the statement. Richard also insisted that Catherine sign as a witness.

The reverend shuddered with a coughing fit. Richard waited for his hacking to subside. When it did not, he reached for a tin cup of water from the nearby pinewood shelf.

"Here, take some water," he said as he turned to the dying man. But he was too late. The reverend had slipped into unconsciousness.

"Is he…" Richard began.

Catherine examined her patient. "No, not yet," she said. "But he will be soon. It's doubtful that you'll get any more information from him before he passes, Inspector."

Richard furrowed his brow. He saw how his disappointment annoyed Catherine, and it placed his feelings into perspective. Guilt filled Richard. He had harried that man for answers in his final moments. Perhaps the inspector could have asked if the man had any final wishes or words, but the critical facts were more important than Corbett's last sentiments. Richard planned to tell himself that for the rest of his life. There had been no time.

"I'm sorry, nurse. I'm just short on answers right now."

"But you're not short on solutions, are you? From what I heard the reverend say, there is a villain of the worst kind running Dawson now. Its police detachment itself has been infected with his sins. As the commanding officer of this detachment, you need to set forth and stop Morgan. Bring an end to this monster, Inspector."

"He's not a monster, Catherine. A monster is a thing to be afraid of. This Morgan is just another man who would have the world believe him to be a monster. He's a man all right. One that doesn't value other people, and who has a talent for mistreating them. And I've dealt with men like him my whole life. He's just bigger than most. And yes, I will break this bastard."

Chapter 2

Richard and Francis exited the infirmary and made their way back to their quarters. Richard checked the parade ground to make certain that no one was paying attention to them. No worries about that. The parade ground was empty.

"Francis, did you check the reverend's dogsled?"

"There was no sled or dogs, Inspector. He must have left them out there on the trail because he staggered into the fort with just his snowshoes. It's a miracle he managed to find his way here from Dawson by himself. That's a hard trail to finish at this time of year, even for an experienced woodsman."

"I wouldn't be so quick to use that word. With him being a clergyman, some might start believing it. It was an act of human desperation that brought him to us, Constable. You would be surprised at what a man can do when his life is in the balance."

The two men parted, and Richard walked across the snow-shovelled path to his quarters. His rank gave him the privilege of having a home to himself. It was of the preassembled type that was often sent north as living quarters. The banks of snow he had packed around its sides for added insulation made it look even smaller.

The house's size and quaintness would have actually made it cozy, if not for the mess inside. He pushed his way past the entrance, which was cluttered with unwashed laundry. The walls hadn't been washed down since Richard moved in. A cigar box sat on the home's only windowsill. He would have left the window curtainless, if not for the fact that he needed to hide all of the untidiness.

Anyone visiting the quarters would have noticed the absence of wall hangings. There were no paintings, photographs, craftworks, or any other adornments, and no musical instruments, no games, or anything that might lift a sad spirit. A bookcase opposite the door gave the home its only shade of charm.

A gun-rack held a German Mauser. The rifle was a trophy from the war in Africa. Richard wondered if he would need it now. He stepped towards it and touched its barrel and, as always, was brought back to that troubled time.

1899 saw the outbreak of the war in the south of Africa. He had served in the Canadian Mounted Rifles, and he had given a good account of himself. Like most of the Canadians who went over there, he had grown up with a rifle in his hands, and his horsemanship had always been excellent. In Africa's open country, he honed these skills. It was the only good thing to come out of that war, he once remarked to his wife. He never bothered to elaborate. Why fight in a war to make the world a better place if you are just going to bring its horrors home to your wife? It was enough that she knew about the jungle fever that almost killed him. They both counted him lucky when compared to almost three hundred Canadian soldiers who never came home.

Thinking about his words to his wife, he turned his mind to Rose. She died only one year into their marriage. An outbreak of typhoid at the fort took her away from him in 1903. A quarantine was placed on the fort. No one was allowed in or out, and the Mounties' role was to enforce the blockade.

He wasn't allowed to stay with her after she became ill. He fought for permission, but his commanding officer insisted that his duty was to the public. The Mounted Police, including him, were sent to range the surrounding wilderness and communities to warn others to stay away from Fort MacCammon. When he should have been with Rose, he was forced to ride away from her. He understood that this was necessary for the welfare of the region, but there was an irreconcilable bitterness that he knew would live in him always.

He had always known that many of the townspeople disapproved of their union, he being white and Rose not. Though Richard never knew how much the people disliked the mixed marriage until her death. So few of them had offered condolences. This injury was deepened by the fact that a fellow Mountie lost his fiancé, a nurse from Quebec, to the same epidemic. Yet, that Mountie was showered with well-wishes and prayers from townspeople and colleagues. A part of Richard had felt betrayed by the community he served.

Following Rose's death, he plummeted into the most desperate sadness he had ever experienced. When he started to shirk his responsibilities and was unable to rise from bed each morning, his fellow Mounties called a doctor. The doctor diagnosed him as suffering from melancholia and treated him with small doses of morphine.

He finally resumed his full duties after a few weeks. Whatever the other Mounties thought of his distress, they never said. He discontinued morphine treatment because he knew that if he stayed on it, it would damage his career and reputation. He used alcohol as a substitute. It wasn't long before it began to devour him.

He always thought it was just a joke; drunks consuming Bay Rum for the alcohol. Then one night, when he couldn't find booze anywhere in his house, it was almost as if he could smell the alcohol in that aftershave. That was the first hint to him that he was developing a problem, but he ignored it.

There were several episodes where his heavy drinking impacted his work and work relations. He remembered the holiday party two years ago. It was the detachment's first Christmas party. Citizens and Mounties alike were invited to mingle and share in the fellowship of the season. He struck a conversation with the wife of an agent for the

Hudson's Bay Company. She had told a joke about a talking pig. It was charming. He could have ended that conversation with a laugh and then excused himself. Instead, the eight glasses of scotch he had consumed emboldened him. He tried to top her joke with one of his own about a nun, a rooster, a duck, and a donkey.

His fellow officers looked on in horror. All faces turned red, and a couple even left the room. That was the last Christmas party held by the Royal North West Mounted Police's detachment at Fort MacCammon.

For a long time after that, the other Mounties worked around him. It wasn't that they disliked him, but he had become a difficulty (and a liability). The easiest way to deal with him, as they saw it, was to simply bypass him whenever they could.

Richard wasn't stupid. He could tell people were avoiding him. Until this point, he had never realized that the Canadian north could get any lonelier. With no one in his corner, he would have to press on alone.

He knew that drunkenness was destroying him, and he recoiled at thinking what Rose would think of him. His shame was magnified because he had heard that overindulgence at the northern posts was a hazard even before arriving here. The rumours were that booze gave Mounties up here relief from the boredom and monotony that so many of them experienced.

The heavy drinking had climaxed six months earlier. Catherine's husband, Constable Walter Sands, dropped by the infirmary to visit her. Walter caught Richard red-handed with medicinal alcohol. He saved Richard some humiliation by not reporting it to any of the other Mounties. He just stared at Richard disgusted, and turned away.

The next day, Richard found a note from Walter left at his desk. The note reported the disappearance of medicinal alcohol from the infirmary and advised the Inspector to "address the matter." Nothing more had to be said. There was something about another person seeing him. Not catching him in the act, but *seeing* him. Seeing him for what he was and how low he had gone. He quit drinking that day.

Abandoning the drink was rough. It never hurt, as such, but it aggravated him in every respect. He never slept well. He would pace around his quarters in the early hours with apprehension coursing through him. When he did sleep, his dreams were plagued with ill thoughts of Africa and Rose.

His heartbeat became irregular and his restlessness couldn't be tamed. He felt as if his muscles were grinding together, waiting to be satisfied by something that his mind now found repulsive.

The good news was that he had been sober for half a year now, and these symptoms had subsided. Sobriety had enriched him beyond expectation. He was not only improved from his state of drunkenness, but enhanced beyond what he had been prior to that. As a drunkard, he had become accustomed to pushing himself each hungover day to achieve a successful standard of performance that allowed him to continue on to the evening's drinking and the next day's hangover. Practice had taught Richard to focus while drunk, to work while dehydrated and hungry, and to learn to see through a fog of booze every one of those days.

Over time, he had trained his clouded mind to concentrate and to handle pressure. His body's coordination and endurance were enhanced by the constant strain of self-abuse. It reminded him of how the body improves from steady physical exercise, or how, in the army, soldiers perform well in the worst of conditions after years of hard training.

Having honed his body and mind to that level, and simultaneously having had the burden of alcoholism removed, he was recast as a superior being. During target practice earlier in the week, he easily bested every other Mountie present. When a larger Mountie challenged him to an arm-wrestling match at lunch, the others were surprised at how easily Richard defeated him.

He was now able to apply himself, this sharpened man, to his work and his life. He spent most of his free time sitting next to the bookcase, reading Kipling. For the first time in a long time, he felt balanced.

But this evening, a crisis had fallen into his lap. Dawson, the crown city of the north, was overrun with thieves. And a reverend, of all people, had been shot. Richard turned his thoughts to the reverend's soon-to-be widow. He told himself that, should he ever meet her, he would lie and say that the reverend's last words were, "Tell my wife that I love her."

He sighed and fell into his cushioned chair. He stared at the Mauser rifle hanging in its rack and wondered what the hell he would do next.

Chapter 3

The men shuffled their feet and cast glances at each other, trying to read each other's minds. Azarov never had any trouble reading them. Their uneasiness hummed through the air. But none of them spoke. Then, Azarov did.

"I know that this was not a part of our plans. I know that we all want to go home. But we cannot leave this business unfinished."

Unfinished due to my poor shot, he thought. And he knew some of the men were thinking the same thing.

"Think about what Morgan will do if we return to Dawson and tell him that we failed."

The group's tension jolted upwards at the sound of the man's name. Azarov knew what they were all thinking now. The Alderman brothers had been a part of the gang, just like any one of them. Now, they were at the bottom of a pond, never to be seen by human eyes again. Morgan's viciousness was becoming more frequent and unpredictable. Some of the men even avoided contact with Morgan, preferring to receive their instructions through Azarov.

"What do you mean exactly?" one man asked. If anyone were to question him, Azarov expected it to be this man. Lang. There always had to be some bastard in the group who made things harder than it needed to be. In this group, it was Lang.

Lang said, "Did you hear me? I want to know what you mean." His tone demanded an answer, but Azarov only shrugged. He preferred to let his comment float in the air and have Lang's imagination do the rest.

"You should be happy that I have a plan," Azarov said. "We don't have time to go over the details now. Just prepare your gear and follow me."

The group broke apart, and the men gathered their packs and weapons. All the while, Azarov stared at Lang. The other men had nicknamed Lang Weasel. With his pointed nose and beady eyes, Lang really did look like one of the damn things.

Goddamn Lang, Azarov thought. *I wonder how much more trouble he is going to give me.* He knew that the men's loyalty was being strained, and that rebelliousness was contagious. With the sort of talk that Lang was putting to them, how long would it be before Azarov would have to face a full revolt?

But he needed Lang, at least for now. His experience on this trail made him the best guide that Azarov could find. Besides, Morgan had assured him, there would be other advantages to having a crooked Mountie in the group.

***

The pot-bellied stove crackled in the corner of Richard's home. He removed the lid and dropped in a piece of birch. Watching the fire's sparks drift upwards to his face, he wished he could stay focused on only them. Instead, he had to face the men standing behind him.

By now, everyone in Fort MacCammon had heard of the stranger who had been shot. He had passed away that night, just as Catherine predicted. Richard had made her promise not to disclose the truth to anyone. Instead, they spread a story throughout the fort. The deceased had been an American big-game hunter who accidently shot himself and, very regrettably, passed away this evening.

"Well, my first hunch about him was as believable as anything we could create," Catherine had told Richard, and he had agreed.

The men behind him were Mounties, and Richard had summoned them to his home to give them the real story of Reverend Corbett, as well as their orders.

Richard pulled off the stove lid and dropped a second log inside. Sparks floated about his face, and a blast of heat forced him to lean away. He felt the men's stares behind him. He finally turned to face them.

"Men, I have called you to my quarters at this late an hour for a good reason. I know the story that you have all heard. The man who died last night was a trophy hunter from the United States. The poor devil discharged his own rifle in a hunting accident. The nurse did everything she could to save him, but, despite best efforts, it was not God's will that he live. Let it be a hard lesson to all that a man should never hunt alone and the safe handling of firearms is always paramount."

A couple of the men nodded, which Richard took as a cue to continue.

"That story is rubbish. I know because I helped to invent it. I made our nurse swear to keep the truth a secret. Thus, you will be the only others who will know the truth. You are to keep it strictly confidential."

Richard then explained the reality of the situation to the men: a murderer needed to be captured, a crook named Morgan had taken control of Dawson, and a gold heist had to be stopped. The men were taken aback by the news. If not for the crackling fire, his house would have been silent. Richard wondered if they would speak at all. He was about to ask them for their thoughts when he was interrupted.

"Do you think that all of what that reverend said is true, Inspector?" Constable Walter Sands said.

"I believe it. I don't want to. The Mounted Police underwent some cleaning fifteen or twenty years ago. Most of the drunks and scoundrels were dismissed. Real order was put to the service. You should have seen what it was like back then. But I'm not foolish enough to think that there's no corruption in the whole service today."

"Some of those Mounties are probably getting two or three times their regular pay!" Constable Robert Donovan said. Richard knew that Robert had some personal financial troubles, so his comment was understandable.

"What about the people? The townsfolk? Can't they stand up to this Morgan? There's the church, the newspapers. Didn't Dawson have some sort of vigilante group years ago?"

"They did. The Vigilance Committee. It did a great job of ridding the town of crime and deviance, but it was disbanded years ago. Now, the citizens are too afraid. They've seen what happens to people who stand up to Morgan."

"So, what's our next move, Inspector?" said Theodore, one of younger Mounties.

"We're going to travel to Dawson. I'm certain that Vadim Azarov has scurried back there after shooting the reverend. We will arrest him and crack that scum Morgan too. We're going to travel to Dawson under the guise of an early Winter Patrol. The patrol would have left Fort MacCammon in a couple of weeks anyhow. Thus, I'll inform the fort that a patrol is departing early because we have some construction at Fort MacCammon planned in the forthcoming weeks, and I want all of the patrolling men back to the fort in time to pitch in.

You've all done the patrol before. Your orders are to prepare your dogs, sleds, gear, and selves. We leave tomorrow morning at eleven. Are there any questions?"

No one asked anything. Richard doubted that they had no more questions. He believed they were too shocked by his revelations to ask.

"Good. Then you're dismissed," Richard said. "Get some rest before the long day, men. And remember, everything I've told you today is confidential. Tell no one, gentlemen."

The men departed, except for one. Walter, one of the men who had spoken.

"May I have a word with you, Inspector?" Walter said.

"Of course, Constable."

Walter waited for the door to shut behind him before he continued. "Catherine is coming with us to Dawson tomorrow."

"I don't take orders from a constable. You would do well to remember your place," Richard said.

"I never gave an order. I stated plain fact. She's my wife. We both know that it's unsafe for her to stay here. She is coming with us."

"I've already taken into account — "

"You've taken into account that Eric Morgan has already infiltrated Fort MacCammon. And you've taken into account that Catherine knows the truth. That puts her in danger, Inspector."

"She'll be fine if she stays here, Constable."

"Is that why you swore her to secrecy? Because what she knows doesn't matter? You owe me, Richard, and I'm calling for payment."

Richard ground his teeth. He never let his men call him by his Christian name. Such informality breeds insubordination and laziness. And for a lower-ranking man to speak to his commanding officer that way was almost unheard of in the Mounted Police. If Walter had said half of this in front of an audience, Richard would have had no choice but to discipline him. Some officers would have even called for his dismissal from the service. However, Walter was smart enough to hold his words for a private moment.

Richard stood up straight and stepped towards Walter. The constable was not a small man, but Richard's six-foot-one frame was not to be discounted. When the constable backed up, Richard's tension eased. Walter had helped to get him away from the drink. Now, Walter was keeping Richard's secret about the reverend.

How many more times will I owe this man? Richard asked himself.

"Don't push your luck with me, Walter. But you're right. I do owe you. If she comes, you'll be the one responsible for her and any harm that befalls her. Am I clear? Good. Then get out of my quarters. Make sure you and your wife are ready to leave in the morning."

After Walter left, Richard stared out the window. The fort was livelier now. People travelled the paths and wooden walkways, trying to busy themselves. Really, they wanted an excuse to be out of their homes and getting the latest news from neighbours.

Let them gossip, he thought. Richard had already set forth the cover story about the dead man. His lie only needed to hold a little longer.

***

The full-length mirror was an embellishment that some may have thought was out of place in Richard's home. Hand carved out of cherry wood, it was a wedding gift to him and Rose. Now, he stood in front of it for a Mountie's self-inspection. He placed his hand on his lower back and leaned back. He groaned as he felt his muscles loosening. All of the fat he had gained on his belly these last few years wasn't helping his back. He patted his mid-section and examined his reflection. It felt, and looked, like it had grown since he had last examined himself.

"Maybe the Winter Patrol will do me some good. The exercise sure as hell couldn't hurt," he muttered to himself.

He checked his attire. "A Mountie needs to ensure that his uniform always looks proper," he would tell Rose. But the Mountie's regular uniform was indisputably useless for the Yukon's winter climate. What good was a Stetson in forty-below conditions? And while the black, leather cavalry boots might look splendid on a parade ground, they did little to keep out the water. Even the proudest Mounties grudgingly confessed that the clothing of the indigenous people was far better than that issued by the service.

Instead, Richard wore non-regulation clothing that was hand-crafted and acquired from the local people. His fur parka with a heavy-trimmed hood was pulled over a wool hat. A suit of caribou hide gave another layer of protection. In addition, he wore seal-skin mitts the size of oven mitts. He always thought they looked more like the gauntlets of some Arctic knight. With his waterproof mukluks on his feet, he could be mistaken for one of the fort's regular citizens.

As Richard loaded his pack, he was mindful of the heavy Colt New Service revolver lying on the bed. The pistol held only six rounds, but those six shots were .455-calibre bullets that hit like little stampeding elephants. The heft of the big-bore gun felt reassuring in his hand, like he was holding real safety. The gun had seen little use in the north. He fired it once to put down a horse with a broken leg. Another time he fired two shots in the air to frighten away a wolf that came too close to his door. Ordinarily, he would curse its weight. It was one more thing to encumber him on a journey where ounces made a difference in a loaded pack. Now, he wondered if he would need it, and, perhaps, if it would be his most important tool of all. He placed it in its holster and strapped on his gun-belt under his coat.

His eyes panned around the room. He would leave the Mauser in its rack. Instead, he chose to bring his Winchester carbine. It had been a favourite with frontier lawmen for decades. The light, short rifle was perfect for long-range patrolling and handling in the underbrush. It never caught on trees as did longer guns. Yet, it had enough punch to drop some big game if their food ran low. Richard pulled his rifle and pack over his shoulders and dropped a full box of cartridges into his pack.

He gave himself one last look in the mirror. He was satisfied that he at least looked ready. Preparation was the best thing one could do to survive the Winter Patrol. Once out there on the trail, all Richard would be able to do was pray for good weather and that there would be little snow between Fort MacCammon and Dawson.

Travelling between spots was one of the most difficult and dangerous tasks for a Mountie in the Yukon. The northern landscape was so convoluted with innumerable winding streams and high hills, it was easy to mistake landmarks. Whiteouts and heavy fog also made it very hard to navigate the trail. Anyone who had ever hit a trail in dense fog knew how easy it was to wander off the right path. Worse, when a traveller could see only three feet in front of him, it was simple to lose his footing on uneven ground and cliffs. At least once a year, Richard heard of another trailman who stepped off the rocks and fell to his death.

Richard sighed. At least he would only be travelling for a few days. He once did the long Winter Patrol, between Fort McPherson in the Northwest Territories and Dawson City. By the end of that thirty-day patrol, he wasn't sure if he was the same person as he was before he started. The Winter Patrol had a way of raising a person to a new level of resourcefulness and resilience. This fake Winter Patrol that now lay ahead wouldn't be anywhere near as hard on his psyche.

He slipped on his fur coat and pulled its fur hood tight over his wool hat. The last thing he did before leaving his quarters was glance at the cigar box on the windowsill. He promised that, when he got back, he would take out the war medals that were inside and find a better home for them.

Chapter 4

Richard was confident that he had selected good men to accompany him. He strode towards the parade ground, eager to inspect them and get the journey underway.

He found the parade ground bursting with excitement. Mounties checked their loads. Sled dogs yelped and snapped at one another. As he crossed the ground, Richard saw a group of citizens to his right. They watched the preparations with amusement. He thought of asking them if they had anything better to do but kept silent. Fort MacCammon had seen more excitement in the last day than it had in the previous three months, or likely would for the next three. So, he decided to let these people enjoy it.

"Good morning, Inspector," Michael Townsend said.

"Constable," Richard replied.

"I hope you're well-rested." The constable's voice had a chirpiness that reminded Richard of the way nurses speak to patients.

The glare Richard gave said it all: *Don't start anything with me, Mike. Not today.* Mike often made snide remarks, but his dislike of Richard had become more intense the last while. Richard knew why.

Eight months earlier, a position had become available with the Dawson City detachment.

"Dawson City has everything," Mike preached to the other Mounties. "Electricity, running water, pretty girls … everything! I'm ready to move there as soon as I get notice."

There was a lot of talk among the men about how Mike was already scouting properties in Dawson — something that would make his wife happy and that he could live with.

And Mike had reason to be sure of himself. His service record was excellent, and one of Mike's friends at the detachment had put in a good word for him. Everyone thought he was a shoe-in for the position. He had written letters to his family back in Kingston, telling them that he was the obvious choice.

All that he needed was for Richard to push through some paperwork. However, Richard had been drinking steadily for three weeks. He kept deferring the paperwork, staying in bed for several days and telling others that he was fighting a bout of illness. The paperwork never went through on time. The position was awarded to another man.

Mike made no effort to hide his anger after his opportunity to move on to bigger and better things had dissolved. What's more, he felt he had made a fool of himself with his cocksure talk.

At the time, Richard had promised himself that he would find a way to redeem himself for what he did.

Mike turned his back to him and continued heaving gear onto his sled. At forty, Mike was barely younger than Richard, and Richard knew that they must share many of the same aches and pains that come with age and hard living in the north. But Mike's toned frame hid them well. He threw a mailbag on top of the sled as if it were only a feather pillow, but Richard knew how much those bags weighed. Then, Mike repeated the action with another bag that was so overstuffed it would not close.

Richard saw the cords of muscle in Mike's neck strain as he lifted that sack, but he handled the load with no complaints.

"Constable, did you get your shotgun, like I asked?"

Mike touched the bandolier of shotgun shells slung over his coat, as if to say the answer was obvious.

"Damn right I did."

Richard looked more closely at Mike's sled and saw the stock peeking out from underneath other gear. The shotgun's opulent stock made it look out of place among the rest of Mike's crude things. It was Mike's prized possession. The double-barrelled shotgun was custom-made for target shooting, but Mike used it often for hunting.

He and Richard went fowling a few times together, and Richard knew that Mike could hit a bird on the wing at almost impossible ranges.

"Anyone who says that you don't have to be a good shot when you're firing a shotgun is wrong, Inspector," he said. "It just takes a different kind of shooting skill."

Richard did not disagree, and he was glad that Mike had agreed to bring the side-by-side, in case they needed to shoot some small game … or anything bigger.

"How many men does Eric Morgan have on his side?"

"A lot," Richard replied. "Maybe twenty. Maybe as many as fifty. We don't know."

Mike opened his mouth and Richard waited for the spiteful comment. Seeing the tension in Richard's face, Mike softened.

"If it comes to it, I'll make every shot count."

"Thank you, Constable."

Richard walked over to Francis, whom he had put in charge of provisioning the patrol group.

"How are we doing with the food, Constable?"

"Hello, Inspector. Please see for yourself. I loaded each item on this list with your specified amounts per person."

Francis handed Richard a list of the food stocks. There was no room on the sleds for luxuries, or what Richard's wife had called "nice-to-haves." The sleds could only carry so much weight, and they had space for only so many supplies. It was essential that every pound of each sled's allowance be used to the greatest benefit. Richard read the list of items given to him. The items included the following:

Tinned milk
Salt
Coffee and tea
Baking powder
Sugar
Dried fruit
Flour
Beans
Butter
Lard
Corned beef
Bacon
Dog food (dried fish)

The food list met Richard's satisfaction. Richard knew that the most important item on that list was the last one: dog food. The dogs powered the sled, and the fish powered the dogs. It was that simple. It never took the Yukon's newcomers long to learn that the only beasts of burden worth owning in this land were dogs. It was too hard to find good pasturage for oxen, horses, or others. Dogs, however, could be well-fed on the wealth of fish that the waterways provided. As a benefit, the little bales of dried fish were lighter and easy to pack in their dehydrated state.

With the addition of firearms, ammunition, tents, candles, axes, the camp stove, blankets, mess kits, and other supplies, they would be loaded heavy, but it was manageable. They would also have to haul hundreds of pounds of mail out of the fort, to make it look like a real Winter Patrol, but Richard planned to store it in the nearest cabin the first chance they got.

No, the load definitely wasn't too heavy when carried between the six men and their sleds.

It would lighten a little each day, he thought.

Richard then remembered the extra cargo — Catherine. She would add weight to the party, and she needed to be provided for. Despite trying to conceal his distress, he let out a groan.

Francis raised his eyebrows at that. "Does it look good, Inspector?"

"Factor in that the nurse will be accompanying us and adjust the list accordingly, Constable." Francis did not hide his surprise, but said nothing more than, "Yes, sir."

Richard grinned at Francis. "Besides, if food runs out, and the men don't bag enough wild game, there are always the dogs."

The frown on Francis' face made Richard grin harder.

Francis said, "Lost travellers eating their own sled dogs out of desperation is just a part of local folklore. No one seems to know anyone who has actually had to do it. Additionally, dog meat is supposedly greasy, tough, and wholly unnourishing. Eating too much of it makes you sick, and those who live on it for days develop sores on their skin and the inside of their mouths."

Richard chuckled at the young constable. "Well, someone has been studying! Relax, Francis. Did you forget that there are a couple of food caches stored along the trail in case travellers need to resupply? We can always use those, Constable. Besides, I doubt if the dogs would mind eating one of their own. If it comes down to dog meat, we'll eat the dog's share of dried fish, butcher one dog, and feed him to the others."

"You've thought of everything, Inspector," Francis said and smiled back.

When he smiled, Richard was reminded of how much he looked like his father. It was Richard's honour to have met Francis Dubois Senior — one of the original Mounties. His father was a point of pride for the younger Francis. How many times had he crowed about his father being one of the first Mounties who made the famed journey out west? There was hardly any need for boasting. His father was a legend in the service for reasons besides that.

His son was not so acclaimed, however. Francis Junior left Halifax and joined the Mounties in 1902, much to his father's pleasure. Francis was first stationed in Kingston, where his father was serving his remaining years before retirement. Richard wondered if that was a coincidence or if Francis Senior had influenced his son's deployment. It must have been a surprise when, after only three years of service, Francis requested redeployment to the Yukon. Perhaps he thought he had something to prove. The prospect of him trying to match his father's reputation was commendable.

However, Francis' true gift lay in administration. There was no stack of reports too high for him to climb. Most officers wrinkled their noses at paperwork. Francis never complained, and, more importantly, he was better at it than most Mounties.

"Every one of us must work to his best advantage," he would say, and who could argue with that?

Richard never wanted Francis to be a part of this journey and would have preferred another man instead. With only five years in the service, Francis was the fort's least seasoned Mountie. This would be only his second Winter Patrol, real or fake. But Francis was the one who brought him the news at the Brownstone about the shot reverend. So, Francis already knew the early Winter Patrol was a hoax. If he stayed at the fort, the truth could leak out.

Besides, Francis was damaged. Eight months earlier, two prospectors from London, Ontario, were travelling northbound to a trading post, but they never reached it. A search party was sent out, and the two men were indeed found. No one saw that as a success, though. The pair had washed up on the side of a fast-moving creek. From the best anyone could reckon, they had hit the rough rapids upstream. Their little wooden boat was nothing more than a flat-bottomed tub, the collapsible kind that could be broken down and packed. The charlatans sold them to the gullible as the easy way to travel through the Yukon.

The boat had collapsed all right, as soon as the hard whitewater struck it, and then the boat had struck even harder rocks. The boat was smashed into splinters, and so were the men. Who knows if it really happened like that, but sometimes people just need to fill in the missing pieces of a story, and it certainly sounded believable. What usually killed the newcomers was a combination of inexperience and lousy luck.

What was certain was that Francis had been one of the party members who found the prospectors. Their ears and lips were missing, and the eye sockets of both men were empty. Crows and other beasts always go for those fleshy parts first. Richard had heard that Francis vomited when he saw the dead men lying on the creek's bank. They had been facing skywards, with no lips to hide their death-grins.

Richard stepped away from Francis, satisfied that he had addressed the worst man in the patrol. Now, it was time to speak with the best. He crossed over to the next sled and its owner, Trapper Jerry. When Richard was first introduced to him, he thought that the man must be a remarkable trapper to earn that nickname in a land filled with trappers. His assumption proved correct. Jerry could catch anything on four legs, which was one of several characteristics that made Trapper, in Richard's view, the most interesting person around Fort MacCammon. He also knew how to speak both English and French, along with the language of his people, making him one of only two people in the whole area who could do all three. Where the old man learned French was something that Richard always wondered about but never bothered to ask. Even though Richard was a man of authority, he didn't need to know everything.

"Good morning, Trapper."

"Same to you," Trapper said. The old man's face was worn and dark like a ballplayer's mitt. Still, his eyes shone with life, and he always showed a liveliness that never reflected his age. He always reminded Richard of a character from a Walt Whitman poem.

"Trapper, how far do you think we can get each day, with the weather being what it has been? Are we likely to see more of the same?"

This made Trapper cackle. "Can't you tell for yourself yet? You've been up here for years."

Richard let the insult slide. After all, Trapper held the status of "special constable," and some pardons came with that. Special constables were not regular members of the police service. They never had the status and training of regular policemen, and the same expectations for behaviour were not applied to them. They were auxiliary policemen meant to supplement the Mounties.

During his years in the north, Richard had befriended Trapper and many other of the Gwich'in — some of the original people of this northern land. Other white men had different words for these people, but Richard saw these terms for what they were: ugly, harmful, and undeserved. There were not many Gwich'in, and the few that there were lay scattered across the Northwest Territories, the Yukon, and into Alaska. It was common for the Mounties to hire the Gwich'in men to serve as special constables. They were well-paid by the Mounties to provide certain services, including hunting and acting as trail guides.

It was through the provision of these services that the Mounties met the land's challenges, and not one of them took the special constables for granted. Cooperation with the people who were native to this land was vital to the successful settlement of the north. Richard respected them for what they were: good people, skilled and knowledgeable, and this land's first inhabitants.

Richard patted Trapper's shoulder. The journey would be exhausting, but Richard was confident that he had a good guide and an able woodsman in Trapper. Richard figured that he might be able to navigate the patrol's way along the trail by himself, but, as a precaution, he wanted to bring a guide. He knew that much of the area was still badly mapped, and there were too many junctions and side trails along the route. Overconfidence kills in the Yukon.

"Well, I figure we can get about thirteen miles each day. It's about forty-three miles from Fort MacCammon to Dawson, so we can do it in three days if we push hard out there," Richard said.

"Twenty-two? I was thinking more like twenty-five."

"Maybe we can get fifteen miles a day, if the weather cooperates. But let's say thirteen miles. I want us to be cautious with our estimates. Things happen out on the trail. Problems happen. Much of the region is still uncharted. There's probably some parts that no man has ever set foot upon."

"Well, that no *white man* has set foot upon," Trapper said and grinned. He looked up and studied the sky, which was filling with clouds. "Speaking of the weather, it's getting worse. I think we should wait for it to pass before we head out."

"No time, Trapper. We move now."

Near the middle of the sled was Trapper's son, Henry. He was lashing gear onto the sled. With the exception of their snowshoes, which dwarfed his, Richard noted that the gear carried by his Gwich'in friends matched his own.

Richard was more interested in Henry than the gear. He had watched this boy grow. Now, in his twentieth year, Henry hardly resembled the child Richard met when he first came north.

"Are you ready for another patrol, Special Constable?" Richard asked smiling.

"You can be sure of it, Inspector. I got the dogs ready. The gear is ready. I'm ready."

"Good man. I'll be lucky to have a solid guy like you next to me when I'm out there on the trail." Richard made sure to say this loud enough for Henry's father to hear it. As he walked away, Richard patted Henry's shoulder. He glanced over to Trapper and saw the old man's eyes smiling. Richard wished he had a son who gave him such pride, but he was still childless.

The cold air was starting to hurt his lungs, and Richard's nose hairs were freezing and getting prickly. He was eager to get moving. However, there were more party members who needed addressing.

Walter and Catherine's sled sat at the far end of the parade ground. Catherine leaned against their sled as she double-checked her food rations. Richard was comforted to see that she was trying to make herself useful. Catherine's auburn hair was hidden under a hat and fur hood. He looked over the rest of her. Richard was satisfied that she was dressed properly for the journey ahead.

"Constable Sands, come here," Richard yelled. He wasn't about to walk over to Walter.

Walter crossed the parade ground with a look on his face that said he knew what was coming. Still, it had to be said.

"Good morning, Inspector," he said.

"To hell with the morning and with you. You've made a big problem much larger with your dismissal of my authority. Do you really need to bring her along?"

"Inspector, I — "

"Shut up, Constable. I wasn't finished speaking. Out on the trail, I'm in charge of everything except for her. She is your responsibility. Remember that."

Richard turned and walked away. His last words to Walter were already feeling untrue when he called to his party.

"Everyone, make your final preparations. We leave in ten minutes. Once we are on the trail, I want us to drive hard. We have roughly six hours of daylight each day at this time of year. I want us to make the most of them."

He saw Mike's wife give her husband a hard kiss. It said, *Goodbye, good luck, and I love you.*

"Bring him back home to me as he is, Inspector Carol," she said to Richard.

Richard gave her a smile that felt disingenuous, though he didn't know why it should. "I'll bring him back in one piece. Everyone's coming back just fine."

As the party's members readied themselves, Richard examined them, re-evaluating his choice of team. He knew that some people at Fort MacCammon, in all likelihood, had already sided with Morgan. Mike, despite his feelings towards Richard, was too loyal to the service to ever betray it. Walter, with his wife now involved, had too much at stake to be a risk himself. Trapper and Henry were outside of the fort's inner circle of Mounties, and so Richard hoped they wouldn't have been chosen to serve as accomplices. Francis was the only one Richard wasn't certain about. However, he already knew too much, and so Richard had to bring Francis along.

He gritted his teeth. In bringing Francis, it was one of the rare times Richard hoped that he was being overcautious.

***

The party pulled away from Fort MacCammon. Trapper led, followed by his son's sled. Richard's was the last. He wanted to be positioned to watch the group. The last thing he needed was for anyone to fall behind or get lost. What was needed was a quick and coordinated drive to Dawson with no complications.

The dogs embraced their freedom from the fort. Prisoners who had been set free to run as they were born to do. Baying. Barking. Yapping. Yelping. They charged forward, not knowing where they were heading and not caring. There was the running. That was all.

From his vantage point, the line of sleds reminded him of a desert caravan. Bucking beasts, heavy loads, and travellers who already looked tired before the journey even began.

He turned back to Fort MacCammon for a last glimpse. He sighed and now saw that the fort that he so disliked was not without its merits. He thought about how good it would be to sit in the Brownstone and enjoy Jean-Paul's latest creation. There would be no moose steak or roasted potatoes on this damn trip.

Ahead of him, he saw the mouth of the trail opening from a treeline made up of pines. The weather had broken some of the weaker trees, crisscrossing them in a strange tangle. When Richard first heard of the trail, he expected a neatly groomed path. Big-city life, with all of its well-travelled walking trails, had placed that image in his mind. But this route was so narrow. So furrowed. If not for the modest effort by his men to axe-cleave a trailhead, he wouldn't have guessed that there was a trail there at all.

Trapper's sled entered the trailhead, and it sprang when it hit a covered rock. The old man stumbled while his sled righted itself. Then he vanished into the trees. The others tailed him without breaking their pace. Now their journey had truly begun.

Chapter 5

The almanacs said that this winter would be warmer, though, from what Azarov could tell, it was just as cold as the winter of 1906 or 1905 or any other year. Crouching by the fire, he warmed his hands. The stink of smoke comforted him. If he could smell the smoke, he thought, at least that meant his nose hadn't frozen off. Azarov smiled. It was nice to know that his sense of humour hadn't frozen. He looked at the men surrounding the campfire and knew he couldn't say the same for them. They looked ready for home, a warm bed, and a shot of rum to take away the chill.

"Do you want some bacon and beans, boss?" a red-haired man, nicknamed "Lottery," asked him. He smacked his lips and licked the grease from his fingers.

"No."

"Why not?" the man said. "You haven't eaten anything today."

"The hungry dog runs the farthest." Azarov smiled again. Two jokes in one minute was rare for him.

"That's an old saying," the man said. "My daddy used to say the same thing sometimes."

Frowning now, Azarov rose to his feet. Without a word, the other men also rose.

"Get yourselves ready. Company will be here soon," Azarov said.

The other man scratched his copper beard and waved his hand at the group of men around him. "Boss, do you really think we needed to bring all these men just to handle this?"

"I think we needed to bring more. I think men desert other men in hard times, and we need a few spare. Why are you all still standing here? Must I tell you twice?"

The men departed, but Azarov decided to linger by the fire for a moment longer. He watched its embers pulse bright and darken. He wondered if Morgan had any idea what he had set into motion when he sent Azarov and the rest of these men to chase down that reverend. Did Azarov himself know?

One thing was certain: There would be plenty of dead bodies to tell Morgan about when Azarov returned to Dawson. Many of those would be Mounties. This saddened him. Azarov had respect for the Mounties, or at least for the service they provided. He had seen how they had saved countless lives. He never held any love for them, but he never held any ill will towards them either. They were only performing the duties of their station. Azarov cursed Morgan for using his wife and daughters as leverage against him. If not for the threats made against his family, Azarov wouldn't have to hurt any Mounties at all.

Azarov loaded his pipe and lit it with a twig that he pulled from the fire. He pulled his bearskin coat tighter to his body. His mind drifted to years earlier — how he had come to this place. Life had been so simple back when he was a sea captain.

When he arrived in the Yukon in 1885, the Klondike Gold Rush was still twelve years away, but northern Canada was already attracting a great deal of outside attention. The fur trade was well-established by that time. Trading posts were sprinkled across this giant white shroud. Trappers, dealers, and agents of Hudson's Bay Company hustled to make a hard-earned dollar from the coveted furs of wolf and fox.

As well, there was plenty of work offshore in whaling for captains like him. *The Clarissa* was a grand, three-masted steamship that was outfitted for Arctic whaling. Its powerful auxiliary engine pushed it through the pack ice, aided by a bow sheeted in iron. A thick oak hull and extra bracing and ribs throughout the ship gave her added protection from the crushing ice.

Life on *The Clarissa* was profitable, if not comfortable, for the fourteen-man crew. In those days, ships had plenty of game to hunt off the Yukon's coast. Due to a lack of regulation by Canada's government, many foreign whaling vessels operated in the Arctic. They took their fill of bowhead whales without a care for taxes, licences, or quotas. For a brief time, the Canadian Arctic was a whaler's paradise.

Azarov could have lived a very different life if that fine ship had a better fate. *The Clarissa* sunk after a drunken engineer let the boiler explode. The blast opened the ship's portside. Freezing water rushed in with a frightening rapidity, and the ship sank in less than ten minutes. Remarkably, no one but the engineer was killed. He was blown to pieces, with chunks of flesh and bone flung far out onto the sea ice. Whenever Azarov told *The Clarissa's* story, he always added, "I would have kicked that drunk's ass if anyone was able to find it!"

Well, that was the story Azarov told to people. It made him sound guiltless. The real fate of *The Clarissa* was very different. Azarov had kept his vessel off the Yukon's coast far too late into the hunting season. By all rights, he should have sailed for Halifax in September in order to avoid the increasing pack ice. In late October, the Arctic Ocean had transformed into a landscape of jagged ice pans.

To most people, the pack ice looked like a cold, endless wasteland that spread across one's entire field of vision. But, if one watched it more carefully, one could see it come to life. Waves lifted the pack ice, giving it rhythm. The thousands of jagged ice pans ground against and buckled on each other, causing some to rise as high as twenty feet into the air. To Azarov, they looked like dragon's teeth. He imagined that great icefield was its own creature … beating, breathing, wanting.

Finally satisfied with his last catch, a fat bowhead, Azarov had decided it was time to head for land. The fast-flowing sea ice gave him some concern, but he found a channel of open water only two miles from shore. Hugging the coast, he continued south. *The Clarissa* was cutting through a bank of fog so dense that the ship's pilot could barely see one hundred feet beyond that ship's bow. Suddenly, a ghostly shape began to form out of the fog.

A moment later, the pilot realized that it was the bow of a northbound vessel. The pilot pulled the ship's wheel to his right with the greatest of urgency. *The Clarissa* bucked and veered starboard. It ran so close to the other vessel that the pilots of both ships saw each other's shocked faces, as if there had been only one pilot staring into a mirror.

The pilot's reflexes saved the whaler from a headfirst collision, but it had sent the ship into an encroaching line of pack ice. The incoming tide had tightened the sea's ice closer to the shoreline. It crept in faster than Azarov had anticipated.

Every crewman on board was thrown to the deck when the ship struck the ice. Yells and hollering mixed with the exploding ice. *The Clarissa* was lodged deep into an icefield that stretched for miles. The icefield's giant pans squeezed against the ship, locking it in place. Azarov rushed to the ship's pilot house and ordered full-steam to break her free. But *The Clarissa* had hit the ice with poor momentum and at a bad angle. The only thing this pushing achieved was a broken propeller blade.

The crew spent the next day hoping for a break in the pack ice and waiting while the propeller was repaired. The saucy cook remarked that they may well be trapped until next summer, but Azarov knew better. He knew what was to come.

That night, the crew heard a groaning that ran the length of the ship. It was soft at first but unmistakable. Was it Azarov's imagination, or did he feel vibrations run through the ship's straining wooden beams? *The Clarissa* was being compressed by the ice. Azarov knew that he had to move quickly or the next whale he would see would be at the bottom of the damn ocean.

"Abandon ship!" he ordered. "*The Clarissa* is driftwood now!"

The crew made their escape in good order and hiked towards shore. After only five hundred feet, they heard *The Clarissa's* planks cave in. The slush bubbled around the ship's starboard side when the ocean rushed in and the ship's pockets of air blew outwards. The pack ice surrounding her turned black from the soot in the coal stores. Azarov saw his ship hemorrhaging black blood and thought about how he had just spent a fat sum of money to outfit her with new rigging. Christ, he could cry. The ship rapidly started to list, but the ice blocked her from rolling over. Instead, she sank stern-first. Her proud, iron-plated bow was the last thing to be seen of that once ice-worthy ship.

It was Azarov's overconfidence that cost him *The Clarissa*. He could tell that some of his crew thought he was foolhardy to stay out so late in the season. None of them challenged him, however. Part of him wished that they had.

Later, Azarov learned that the approaching ship had been a coastal survey ship tasked with meteorological and tidal studies. He took some relief in knowing that the captain of the survey ship made some of the same blunders. He couldn't fault the captain for poor navigation. The huge migration to the Artic meant that there were plenty of captains who were unfamiliar with the Arctic waters and too many inexperienced crewmen who never knew their work. Sadly, *The Clarissa* became one of many Arctic shipwrecks from those days. What truly angered him was that the survey vessel never stopped to give aid to the ice-stricken *Clarissa*. Azarov had to wonder what was wrong with some people.

Following the sinking, he stayed popular among the former crew. No doubt, he had been a stern captain and could be cruel at times. Whatever reservations other sea captains had concerning corporal punishment ended on his gangplank. However, the men were generously paid and always paid on time. Several had sailed with Azarov for years. Consequently, many of them followed Azarov after *The Clarissa* went down.

Of course, those that followed him were the ones who had few valuable skills for sale once off the waves: the regular seamen, the cabin boy, and so on. They were a rough lot — petty criminals and hard cases, who were a natural fit for working in almost inhumane conditions. Those crew members who had more valuable trades and education (like the ship's carpenter, engineer, and purser) were always in demand among employers.

In 1897, Azarov led his former crew through the north. They arrived in Skagway, near Dyea, on Alaska's west coast. There, he was witness to the Gold Rush. Prospectors had returned to America loaded with gold from the Yukon's Klondike region. They reported that there was still so much more of it up there, just sitting on unowned land! Anyone with a few tools and the initiative could travel to the Yukon and scoop up one bucketload of nuggets after another, or fill flour sacks with gold dust. The only thing that kept a Kansas farmer from being as rich as a Rockefeller was a lack of will. A factory worker from Toronto could take what little money he had in his threadbare pockets, travel to the Klondike, and, a few months later, be as rich as a king! Rarely in human history had this been seen: groups of regular people getting rich overnight.

The American West may have been played out, but it was a new day, with a new frontier, and that frontier lay to the north. Once those prospectors reached America, it took only days for word of the unclaimed gold sites to spread across the world.

For the west, the stampede to the Yukon was an economic godsend. The port cities of Vancouver, Seattle, and San Francisco all saw great influxes of travellers wishing to get outfitted with equipment and to purchase passage to the north. Hotels and restaurants overflowed. Outfitters sold their wares at enormous prices. There weren't enough ships on the west coast to ferry everyone to the

Yukon. A booming press and advertising industry fuelled their excitement. Land surveying and Arctic expeditions also became big business. Now that massive piles of gold had been found, the Government of Canada discovered a new interest in the north, as did foreign powers. Everyone began working themselves into the Yukon's Gold Rush, but not all of them were doing so lawfully.

There were always the swindlers looking to make a quick buck from the fortune hunters. Most of these prospectors were novices who had spent almost no time living rough in the wilderness. They ranged from poor farmers to poorer salesmen. Many well off and better educated people also followed the siren song. Teachers, college boys, and successful business owners dropped their affairs for Yukon gold. After buying their Klondike shovels and their Klondike hats, these rubes set north.

The fortune hunters came as a stampede. One hundred thousand strong, from Paris, New York, Vienna, and everywhere. The gold could be had by anyone ... or so they believed. A person never needed knowledge of mining, special equipment, large amounts of money, or extra hands to help.

Soon, an armada of ships unloaded people and goods onto the shores of Skagway where they formed a tent city. The accidental city was a maze of landed boats, kits, and fresh-cut wood. Pathways wound between tents and clotheslines, leading to dead ends and sometimes looping for no reason at all. Former office workers, shop girls, and factory men blundered about in this community that they were building by the moment. And the whole of the Skagway maze was electrified by the anxiety of its dreamers, howling dogs, and whinnying horses.

It was there that Azarov and his men settled, as much as one could settle in a tent city. They set up a simple outfitter tent on the shores. Most of these people stampeding to the Yukon goldfields either lost their supplies, had them stolen, or never packed enough in the first place. Azarov had heard it all. A snowstorm buried your frying pan and you couldn't find it? A stream soaked your food and you had to throw it away?

By the time they reached Skagway, Azarov was waiting to sell these stampeders the necessities at huge costs. Candles cost six dollars a box — five times their price in Chicago. A shovel or pickaxe cost ten times the going rate in San Francisco. And seventy-five cents for only a pound of onions!

"The miners think the gold is in the ground, but the true gold is within them," he told his gang.

It never bewildered him that so many people were content to pay these prices. To them, that was just the cost of getting a seat at the world's biggest poker table. While paying for their goods, the prospectors could never resist the urge to talk about how it would all pay off. Whenever one of them said they would hit pay dirt, he thought, "Oh, you'll hit some dirt all right. You'll hit some dirt and nothing else."

Missionaries had set up a chapel tent across a pathway from Azarov's outfitter tent. They were looking to do work in the Lord's name. They had no trouble making a congregation out of the tent city's residents. Many were desperate for whatever mercy and sanctuary could be found. The missionaries knew what sort of business Azarov ran and once accused him of exploitation. "Anyone who believes the devil holds a pitchfork," a missionary once said, "never bought a shovel from you."

It all came to an end when a dispute between Azarov and another Skagway outfitter led to that man getting cut. Azarov's antler-handled knife slashed the man open like a bag of flour. He lived, but such an offence meant that a warrant was issued for Azarov's arrest. The warrant was rescinded when one of the captain's former crewmen claimed that he was the knifeman. No one questioned the confusion. Everyone was content with an open-and-shut case. Still, Azarov sensed that it was his time to move on. Azarov was happy to leave Skagway. *It is a miserable place*, he thought. *No one ever smiles there.*

While Azarov made his own fortune, the prospectors headed off for the goldfields. They still had dreams that the gold could be had by anyone. The truth was that the Yukon was more difficult and dangerous than almost anyone anticipated.

Beyond Skagway lay the White Pass, a miserable mountain pass littered with dead beasts and insane people. Few creatures could climb its slopes and makeshift bridges. Even fewer could handle its exposure to the elements. Too many people who had never carried a pack in their lives tried to make it through to the goldfields beyond. Azarov never travelled the White Pass himself, but the defeated people who came back from there talked about corpses half-hidden in the frozen mud or wrapped against tree trunks and exposed roots. Most of those who returned ended up poorer than they had been before they reached the Yukon. If they were lucky, they found passage on a steamer back to Seattle, now broke, and broken in every other sense.

As for Azarov, he and his men, now smaller in number, found themselves in Dawson City. It had become the permanent supply centre and transportation hub that served the prospectors who mined the nearby goldfields. In Dawson, Azarov saw wealth made faster than he had ever seen before.

Like anyone with newfound wealth, the people in Dawson spent their money on luxuries and overindulgence. Their gold nuggets flowed into the town's businesses, both legal and illegal. There were saloons, brothels, dance halls, hotels, theatres, and all manner of other places for weary miners to enjoy themselves. By squandering their money on cheap things sold for more than their worth, the prospectors spread the wealth to the rest of Dawson's citizens. A pretty saloon waitress with a little charm could make more than the average Montreal lawyer. A bartender could make as much as a Vancouver doctor. Where else in Canada could that be said? Where else in the world?

There was plenty of deviance, but it was controlled deviance. Paradise Alley had its brothels and Front Street had its gambling halls, but they were all monitored and regulated by Dawson's detachment of the North West Mounted Police. As long as no one was seriously injured and property remained undamaged, businesses were free to run. Of course, if they found out that a place's games were rigged, then there would penalties.

It was in this thief's town of thieves that he first met Eric Morgan. The man had built a saloon with a canvas roof and a sawdust floor. Wooden stumps served as the furniture, and occasionally, as weapons. His saloon was one of about a dozen in Dawson at the time, and as hard as it was to believe, it wasn't the worst. Not unlike Azarov, Morgan made his coin robbing the fortune seekers.

In those days, Morgan wasn't always so quick to use violence. Money always spoke loudly and persuasively. Those people Morgan couldn't pressure, he either made his business partners or simply bribed. Violence was always a last resort, but he used it on occasion. That never surprised Azarov. A man never got to be the boss of a town like Dawson without cutting a few throats along the way.

Azarov only recalled one false step: the time Morgan was fined for selling spoiled meat at his saloon and for failing to keep a sanitary "kitchen," the kitchen being a pot and ladle kept in the driest corner of the saloon. He received a forty dollar fine and ten days of chopping wood on the police woodpile.

The thing that always leapt into his mind whenever he thought of Morgan was his wedding band. The band itself was nothing special. It was just a gold band. What struck Azarov was that the band was there at all. Morgan's wife had died years ago, but he never seemed like the tender type who would wear it for sentimental reasons. Azarov once heard that Morgan's wife died of cancer. The man never once spoke of her to Azarov, but he liked to imagine that Morgan's wife had been a kind and loving woman.

The best thing that ever happened to Morgan. Azarov was glad that she was not alive today to see the sort of man that Morgan had become.

Soon after the two men met, Morgan offered Azarov a job at the saloon. The Russian's English was good enough to gain him a position as a card dealer. His fearlessness and tolerance for violence soon landed him other opportunities. It turned out that his earlier years spent in the army and whaling had paid a dividend. Like fighting and whaling, hurting people for Morgan was unpleasant work. But, in this world, a man needed a fat bank account, and Morgan paid well.

Azarov asked if he could bring some of his former crew. He still felt some responsibility for them, that he owed them something after he endangered their lives on *The Clarissa*. Though his conscience was small, Azarov still had the need to scrub it clean once in a while. Morgan agreed to let the former crewmen join the gang, but he didn't hide his concerns about who they would be loyal to.

After the Gold Rush peaked, the town's prosperity quickly plummeted. Most of the stakes had been stripped of gold by then, while there were new gold strikes starting elsewhere. By 1899, the Gold Rush was finished. The days of men getting one hundred dollars of gold from one pan of pay dirt were over.

The flurry of activity that had made Morgan and many like him wealthy had finally ended. Many of the card sharps, confidence men, and hustlers left on their own initiative. Those who did not were run out of town by its growing citizenry of decent people. Old Dawson City was a fine playground for rowdy men, but no one wanted to raise a family there. Things had to change, and Morgan recognized that he could either change with the times or be swept away by them. His enterprises, at least from the outside, had to appear as civil as the new Dawson.

His saloon blossomed into a gambling hall, complete with a French chandelier and fine furniture. Such a place was a way for him to keep his ear to the ground, and it kept his rough-and-tumble men happy and close to him.

He invested in some other respectful businesses. He had purchased six lots, not far from Front Street, where the land was too expensive. He tried to buy there but lost while bidding against other business owners. A theatre and a hardware store were built on the land he wanted for himself. He was reminded of his defeat every day when he walked past these businesses on his way to his own.

That year, Front Street was once again transformed. A blaze started when a dancing girl broke a lamp. It almost destroyed the entire street. Many of the buildings that were not scorched were purposely blown up, as the citizens needed to destroy the fire's route to the rest of the town. Dynamiting them was the quickest way. Morgan smiled when that theatre and hardware store were dynamited and their shattered walls were dragged out of the fire's way. What luck he had! Morgan seemed to be clothed in it. Afterwards, he watched the smoldering street and howled with laughter.

To think, all that devastation was probably caused by a girl in a chorus line dancing the cancan. Azarov was always suspicious that the fire was no accident. Maybe Morgan paid to have that lamp knocked over.

"It was a very convenient fire," Azarov once said to Morgan. He hoped to entice some response from Morgan, but he received none.

In any case, the fire had no lasting impact. Front Street was rebuilt in a matter of months. A year after the fire, a new resident couldn't even tell that it had happened.

But, by then, Morgan had become the king of Dawson. He had a sizable gang, predominantly American hardcases mixed with a couple of Azarov's men from his whaling days. In one way or another, they had all travelled to the Yukon to prosper, and one way or another, ended up in Morgan's rough company.

Soon, he was running everything, both legal and illegal. Azarov searched for the word that educated men used …

monopoly. *What an amusing word for such a stern thing,* Azarov thought.

But Morgan had changed over the last few years, and for the worse. Morgan now bloodied his own hands often. And it seemed he occasionally did it only to demonstrate his propensity for viciousness. It was clear to Azarov that Morgan meant to convey a point. He was saying to people, *Watch out, boys, I'm still the most dangerous man in the room.*

Azarov had seen more violence from Morgan in the last six months alone than he had in the previous five years. The gang had killed and dumped three townspeople into a pond just outside of Dawson. Three! The men now called it Deadman's Pond, which, to Azarov, was a hint that they should start dumping bodies someplace else.

All three victims had been killed on the shoreline of the pond. Crying. Begging. Morgan himself even pulled the trigger for two of them. He gave one man a shotgun blast to the chest at only five paces. The poor bastard's spine was blown out his back.

Later, the men weighted the body and rowed it to the middle of the pond. Morgan smoked his pipe and supervised from the shoreline. "Couldn't he have killed him neater than that?" one of the men later complained while flicking fragments of bone from his boots.

"No, Morgan wanted it to be a mess. Very bloody," Azarov said.

Azarov could see where this was heading. He had a wife and two daughters, and he never wanted to see them scorched by Morgan's growing flames. After several months, Azarov felt it was time to move himself and his family out of Dawson and to Vancouver. He had a brother there who was a stevedore, and he promised he could find Azarov work on the docks.

When Morgan learned of Azarov's intentions to leave Dawson, he was outraged. He glared at Azarov from behind his mahogany desk, with his obnoxious cigar burning in the tray.

"You're too important to the business now, and you know far too much about it to leave. Think twice before you try to walk out on me, Vadim. You have a lovely wife and wonderful daughters. No one wants to see them hurt by your poor decisions."

Azarov had killed much tougher men for doing far less than threatening his family. But he wasn't ready to take the chance. Though he wanted to, Azarov didn't touch Morgan as he sat there. Morgan always had a plan in place to save his ass. He wouldn't threaten Azarov if there wasn't a loaded gun under that desk or a guard standing in the doorway behind Azarov, with knife already in hand.

So now, Azarov and his family were trapped in Morgan's monopoly that Azarov had helped the bastard to build. Worse still, there were fewer and fewer safe places left to stand.

A snowflake caught in his eye, and he blinked out the water. He looked up and saw that the sky was full of the kind of fat flakes that lazily drift to the ground.

He inhaled a long draw from his pipe. The smoke burned his throat and lungs, but, like the campfire, it comforted him. He kicked snow over the last of the fire, not that it needed covering in this weather. But it was a habit of his, and he hated leaving things unfinished.

He agonized over not having caught the reverend on the trail. It would have been so much easier for his party if they had. They could have killed him and dumped his body into some unnamed creek, never to be seen again. People wouldn't have even known he had been murdered, much less suspect by whom.

Lottery returned to the fire and stood next to Azarov. "Boss, the men are ready to move whenever you are. Just give the word," he said.

Lottery then patted Azarov on the shoulder, a gesture that would have been unwelcome coming from some of the other men. But Lot was one of those faithful men who had followed Azarov from his whaling days. Azarov trusted him to follow orders and see a job well done. When a situation boiled into a crisis, Azarov wished that he had more reliable men like him.

And who knows, maybe Lottery really does have some sort of magic luck, Azarov thought. Lot had been a crewman aboard *The Clarissa,* and, one night, he was washed over the side during heavy seas. Falling into the North Pacific during a storm was a death sentence for just about anyone. But the fortunate bastard fell into one of two small wooden boats that had also been washed over the side of the ship only moments before. After that, every time something good happened to him, the other crewman swore that Lottery had the devil's luck, or the luck of the Irish, or some other superstitious nonsense.

Azarov's mind turned to the other unfinished business. By now, the Mounties were undoubtedly on their way to Dawson. He imagined them skirting across a snowfield towards two bridges that lay over a pair of narrow ravines. They were each made of about ten birch logs, each log forty feet in length. They were fixed together, side by side, with small boards laid perpendicular to the logs and nailed into place. It was wide enough for one man and his dogsled to cross at a time. Azarov would lay a trap for them at the bridges — a masterful ambush that would surely kill every Mountie. All he had to do was wait.

Chapter 6

Richard gasped. The dogs pulled while the party's members walked and jogged alongside the sleds, letting the exercise warm them up and giving the dogs some relief. For the third time on the journey, he cursed himself for not keeping in better shape. If only he had quit the heavy drinking months earlier. That may have made all of the difference.

At least the dogs were quiet now. Their excitement at being away from the fort had faded, and so had their yapping and woofing. It was quiet enough that Richard could hear his sled slashing through the snow. That was the sound of progress. The journey was still in its first day, and they were making excellent time. With five dogs for each sled, and six sleds in the patrol, their loads were light.

As well, the region had seen only two moderate snowfalls thus far into the season; it could be much worse. A white cloth draped across the forest floor, but the colossal snowbanks that were seen in the stormiest of winters were absent. On the trail, they had come across the reverend's snowshoe prints and spots of blood from the night before, though they were quickly being veiled by the new snow that was falling. He guessed that, in a couple of hours, these traces would completely vanish from sight. No one with a human nose would be able to tell that a man had bled his way through there.

The men took turns at breaking trail. None of them expected Catherine to assist with this task. Now, it was Walter's turn to be in the front, beating and crunching down the snow ahead, making the way easier for those following. He stopped to move aside one of the dead trees that littered the trail. It was probably the victim of a gale. Though he was still positioned at the back of the group, Richard could hear Walter cursing as he struggled with the obstacle. He prevailed, casting the thin pine to the trailside and clearing the party's way.

They passed a Gwich'in village on the way. It was one of the few left on this part of the trail. Once Fort MacCammon began blossoming into small town, many of the Gwich'in moved there.

When the villagers waved and called to them, the party's members reciprocated. But the villagers were surprised when the party did not stop to rest. Richard had given orders to pass by without halting. Stopping would mean questions, and questions were distractions. It was best not to let distractions become part of their routine. His party needed to stay focused on its task. They passed two cabins as well, the homes of fur trappers. More waves and greetings were given while the sled's slashed onwards.

"Things are going well!" Francis cried.

"Yes, they are, Constable," Trapper said. "But don't let overconfidence set in. That breeds disaster. All it takes is one wrong turn on the route to get an entire patrol lost and dead. Mother Nature is the boss, and she wants to kill you. That's the most important rule out here. Many times, I've completed the Winter Patrol, and I know it. There's no place for a cocky Mountie on the trail."

"Listen to him, Constable. Trapper isn't wrong about any of that!" Richard called from the rear.

The Yukon is a hard land that breeds hard everything: hard beasts, hard men, hard luck, and hard times. Richard thought the police officers posted there had to be equally tough. If not, they would surely freeze to death on some wind-torn snowfield or drown in one of the whitewater streams that marble through the black forests.

But this place would reward the few people strong enough to endure its landscape. It was like campfire smoke that stings the eyes and nose before the fire finally gives its needed heat.

The woods always have a crisp smell of newness, even in the dead of winter. Bars of sunlight pierce the canopies of those dark forests, wounding the ground with white light. Beautiful. Finally, in the quiet of the woods, a lonely peace is always found. To Richard, it was as if God had made this place and said, "*This* is the church that I wanted you to have."

He awoke from his daydreaming when his sled tipped to the left. He cursed and struggled to right it. He finally managed to level the sled by shifting his weight, as he had been taught. Richard had had difficulty learning how to drive a dogsled. Well, more accurately, how to handle the dogs that pulled the sled. It was the little things like harnessing the dogs, marshalling them together, settling them when they were excited, and, sometimes, just getting them to listen. Richard had no trouble with horses, but, with his dogs, he always felt like the bad coach of a good sports team. He had little alternative, however. Dogs were a necessity.

Ahead, Walter had climbed a snowdrift higher than himself. He tossed some deadwood from the trail and called to the rest of the group.

"This drift is much too deep. We will have to double-up," he said.

The others needed no explanation, but Catherine looked at her husband with confusion.

Walter said, "They're going to untie three teams of dogs from their sleds and retie them to the other three sleds. With double power, the dogs will be able to pull the sleds over the snowdrift."

"Then, they'll tie all the dogs to the three remaining sleds and have those pulled over as well," Catherine finished.

Walter smiled at her, happy to see she caught on. "Correct, my love. It should only take the party half an hour to do it all."

It was tiring work. Richard could almost hear his hamstrings groaning under the strain. On the other side of the snowdrift, Richard called a break. Some of the men immediately loaded up their pipes with tobacco and started smoking. Again, Richard was glad he quit smoking a pipe.

His left lung began to hurt. An ache leftover from his many years of smoking, he was sure. Whenever he exerted himself too heavily, the small ache would start to sear; he wondered if it would ever fully disappear. He drew a deep breath and let the crispness of the Arctic air soothe it.

It wasn't long after that they came upon what Richard was waiting to find — the reverend's sled and dogs. Richard's party could hear the dogs barking long before they were seen. And those dogs could hear them. The dogs' excitement grew as the party approached. Their barking climaxed when the first sled came into their view. Whether they were frightened or happy to have visitors, Richard couldn't say. The reverend had left his sled and dog team before a fallen pine tree.

"Looks like he couldn't manage the sled past the tree, so he decided to make it the rest of the way by himself. If only he had some extra hands with him to help."

The group easily shouldered the tree to the side of the trail and then set to the task of searching the sled for anything of importance. They found nothing. His gear looked the same as that of anyone else, except for the leather-bound Bible snuggled into a waterproof sack.

"Unharness the dogs and leave the remaining dog food on the ground for them. Once it's finished, they can have a chance at running wild and finding some more."

The men did so, and the dogs tore into the bales of fish with such ferocity that Richard was sure that they were occasionally biting each other. While the dogs ripped into food, which did not look like it would last long, Richard and the rest of the group began unpacking the sacks of mail.

"Load them onto the reverend's sled and make sure that they're covered. We can pick them up on the way back." Everyone smiled at the thought of lighter loads.

***

At lunchtime, they took refuge in one of the many abandoned police posts that littered the Yukon. While these served well during the boom years, with the depopulation of the area, they quickly fell to disuse. This one, like most, was still fairly new — perhaps only ten years old. Travellers used it as a temporary shelter.

Better still, the men were not snapping at each other the way Richard anticipated. These trips wore on nerves, and, after a little travel, good friends turned into annoying companions. However, his travel mates showed nothing but comradery. Richard counted himself lucky to be in such fine company.

The party had a fire going immediately, and a pan full of corned beef soon hissed over that fire. A little of the dried fruit served as a sweet treat to keep their spirits up. The group gobbled down their meal with all of the enthusiasm that could be expected from exhausted travellers. It seemed like no one would even speak during the meal. Richard was glad when someone finally did.

"Inspector, you mentioned that the man who shot the reverend was named Azarov?' Francis said. "I've never heard of him, but you have, right?"

"Yes, he's a former whaling captain from Russia. His vessel, *The Clarissa*, hunted off the Yukon's coast and that of the Northwest Territories," Richard said.

"It sounds like you're fairly familiar with him. Have you ever had a run-in with this man?"

Richard watched the smoke stir out of the young constable's pipe and thought for a moment before answering.

***

Richard had met Azarov once, two years earlier, in 1905. His first assignment in the north was on board a government ship, the *Marco Polo*. It was tasked with Arctic exploration.

With no background in seamanship, Richard could offer little to earn his keep (a point of resentment from the ship's crew). The fact that he was a unilingual Ontarian and most of the crew were French Canadian did not help him either. Still, travel by this vessel was one of the best ways to police the north. It was relatively comfortable, quick, and it gave him an excellent vantage point from which to regulate Canada's northern whaling and fishing. It was in this capacity that he connected with Azarov.

The Marco Polo had traced the Yukon's coast until the shoreline yawned open to grant access to a small inlet. It was almost invisible upon approach, reminding Richard of some sort of pirate's hideaway from centuries ago. A whaling station was perfectly positioned inside this small inlet. The shoreline was closed on both sides by natural rock walls that were topped with pointed cliffs. These walls protected the station and vessels from foul weather and some of the drifting ice. The inlet's deep water gave good anchorage for vessels, and, perhaps best of all, the inlet was close to the hunting grounds. The whaling station also served as a shelter for whalers in the off-season. Many of those whalers slept on their ships, but some had built sod houses and tar-roofed shacks.

Richard remembered the station well, as it was something experienced through all senses with resounding clarity. A person could smell it long before it was seen. The fatty air around the station would catch in the back of his mouth, making his esophagus tighten.

This greasy place was home to roughly one hundred and fifty whalers, plus a few families. The few houses, along with an Anglican mission and small whalers' cemetery, surrounded the station's core buildings. These were a warehouse and slaughterhouse where the blubber, meat, bone, and hides were taken. Richard recalled the giant dogs that roamed the station's grounds.

He knew that by scouting the station he would find a few whalers without whaling licenses. He could discuss the issues with their captains and perhaps even issue some licenses and accept payments for them on the spot.

Richard saw Azarov's ship, *The Clarissa*, tied at the end of a dock. On the long walk down the dock, he had time to study the man whom he assumed to be the captain.

He saw a squat man with a thick chest and shoulders hidden under a grey sweater. The man was giving instructions to three of his ship's company while they loaded wooden barrels of supplies.

A thin, ragged beard hid some of Azarov's sharp features. His hair was rough and matted down, like that of a wolf. Richard had seen drawings of Genghis Khan and the Mongol hordes and was reminded of them.

Azarov was busy running his men, but, when Richard opened his mouth to announce himself, Azarov turned to him. The Russian's dark eyes locked with Richard's blue eyes. Startled, Richard floundered to explain the need for a license and the fee to Azarov. The Russian captain seemed agreeable enough. Even friendly.

Azarov chuckled. "I should refuse to pay and retire from whaling. It is not what it once was in these waters."

Azarov's eyes broke away only twice. First, they dropped to look Richard over. *He's sizing me*, Richard thought. It was a bad sign. It usually meant that the other man wanted to fight and he was evaluating to see if he could take Richard.

The second time was near the end of the conversation. Azarov's eyes drifted towards a stack of boathooks leaning next to a wooden barrel, and Richard knew the captain wanted to hurt him. He watched Azarov's hands closely, knowing that if they reached for one of those hooks, he would only have a moment to draw his gun and shoot.

Richard noticed that one of those hands bore a heavy scar. Whatever had punched through one side of the hand had gone clean through the other. It was definitely a bullet wound. Richard wondered how well someone who took a bullet through the hand like that could use the hand afterwards. Richard watched that hand until it finally extended to shake Richard's own.

"Of course, there are no bad feelings, yes?" Azarov said while stepping forward. He smiled and Richard returned this politeness. His smile dropped when he caught Azarov's scent. The captain had a musk of body odour, sweat, but also something else. Something visceral, like old blood in hospital bed sheets that no one had bothered to launder. The inspector was glad when the two men at last parted company.

***

Richard finally snapped from his memories and remembered the constable's question. "Yes, I met him before, Francis."

"So, what's he like?"

"Dangerous, Constable. It's difficult to describe him, but I doubt if you will ever meet another person like him. For now, let's just say that he is dangerous and leave it at that, shall we?" Richard said. "If you wish to worry about something, you can worry about the daylight. Remember, we only have five or six hours of it each day, so we need to make the most of it."

Francis smiled. "Well, there's one good thing about this trail in winter — no mosquitoes!"

Richard smiled then, not because the joke was funny, but because he saw the young constable was trying to endear himself to Richard. "Yes, you're right, Francis."

***

The next two hours were uneventful. The group raced along the trail. Its members never spoke. This suited Richard since the dogs' yelping never ceased. Clouds were thickening overhead, and he wondered if there was a storm brewing inside of them. Along with driving a team of dogs, reading the northern weather was also difficult for him.

He trembled against the wind's bite. Richard realized he could hardly feel his toes. There were pins of cold in his toe tips, and he was grateful for the sensation. Didn't they say frostbite had not yet started if a person could still feel pain? He had heard that. Total numbness was the telltale sign. What followed was freezing to death. People always said that it was like falling asleep, but he'd always wondered how the hell they would know. Richard had found people frozen to death before: hunters, travellers, lost children ... They usually went missing close to the settlements from which they had left — certainly not as deep into the woods as Richard was. It might be months until they find his body. He suddenly had an image in his head of his body being found during the spring thaw, all soaking and picked over by the scavengers. He shuddered again, but this time, it wasn't because of the cold.

They crossed a snowfield that stretched twelve hundred yards. The wind charged down a valley to the patrol's right, and battered against them. Richard shivered and fantasized about a cup of hot coffee. He was glad he packed an extra pair of socks. Here, at the end of the snowfield, the trail cut through sizable hills. They would be a most welcome windbreak and make this a good place to set up camp.

Richard guessed that it was about 2 p.m.

"It will be sunset soon. Let's stop here for the night," Richard called.

The party halted and began setting up camp. Everyone was tired, but they still had work to do. The men stripped the limbs from the tree trunks. It was extra effort to make pine-bough beds, but they were warmer to sleep on than the snow, and they were softer than sleeping on the ground.

Richard surveyed the hill pass while the others unpacked, studying the steep slopes covered in willow and pine trees. It was clear that they would help to protect from the wind. The hills were close enough together that only four men, walking abreast, could pass through at once. The narrowness made him uneasy. Africa was far away, but this was the sort of place where the Boers would have set an ambush for Canadian soldiers.

"This looks like a perfect place for a trap, doesn't it, Mike," Richard said.

Mike stopped unstrapping his gear and looked at Richard with surprise.

"Thinking of Africa, Inspector? If I had the time to think of Africa, I would think about its heat. But I don't have time for daydreaming at the moment. I need to help make camp."

Mike went back to work, leaving Richard to feel idiotic. Richard gazed at the others to see if they had caught the conversation. He saw Walter and Francis exchange nervous looks. He could tell they were afraid that Mike had pushed his superior too far, but Richard was ready to let the rebelliousness slide.

Henry had completely missed the exchange and was busy liberating a metal flask from his sled. He took a mouthful of its contents and wiped his lips. Then Henry held out the flask to Richard.

"Do you want a belt, Inspector?" Henry asked. His question was innocent, but Richard could feel the eyes of everyone else on him.

"No, thank you," Richard said and sensed their relief. They didn't trust him yet, and he knew that it would take a long time to earn their confidence.

Before supper or setting tents, the men tended to the critical task of caring for the dogs. Any unusual behaviour in the dogs, such as difficulty barking or breathing, whining, or loss of appetite, was noted. As well, each man checked his sled dogs' paws for cuts and cracking and inspected their mouths, looking for signs of sickness. A sled dog with nice, pink gums was a healthy sled dog. If they were red, white, or blueish, it could mean a host of problems, like blood loss or infection.

One of Henry's dogs was limping. His left forepaw was bloody.

"Shoot him," Trapper said to Henry. His son stood still. Richard understood Henry's hesitation. He had often seen

Henry around the fort with this particular dog. It was a working dog, but it was as close to a pet as Henry had ever had. He had raised that dog since it was a pup, and it was one of his favourites. Shooting it would be nothing like taking a game bird or a rabbit.

The others were surprised when Trapper, without any signal, levelled his own .30-30 rifle at the dog and placed a bullet through its left side. The big dog jumped but made no sound. Its eyes closed a second later, and it was done. Through the whole thing, Trapper never once looked at his son.

Chapter 7

Over supper, the men scooped beans and bacon into their mouths.

"Having a lady present doesn't improve your table manners, I see," Richard said.

Embarrassment crossed their faces, but it turned quickly into relief when Catherine grabbed a strip of bacon and chewed it with her mouth open and grinning. Richard chuckled at her. That was one of the things that he liked about life in the Yukon. Codes of etiquette were more relaxed here. Still, Richard hated having a woman out on the trail in December. He still thought Walter was wrong about bringing her. In all likelihood, she would have been safer back at the fort. Richard had been a fool to let her come.

He looked again at Catherine, and, for the first time since they had left the fort, Richard felt something more than resentment towards her. Like him, it wasn't her fault that she was pulled into this tangle. But unlike him, it was not her duty to untangle the mess. She was a victim of circumstance.

Richard looked over at Walter and saw that the constable had caught him staring at his wife. Richard couldn't blame Walter for wanting to bring her along. He probably would have done the same thing if he were in Walter's place. Richard nodded to Walter, and, when Walter nodded back, Richard knew he'd received the message.

"Excuse me, Inspector," Francis said. "Back there on the trail, you mentioned Africa. If you don't mind me asking, why don't you ever really talk about it?"

Richard sighed. Though, in truth, he didn't mind Francis asking. On the trail, boundaries around personal affairs always fell by the wayside.

"It's all right, Francis. I don't talk much about the war because there isn't much to say about it. Some people there thought it would be a fine thing to have freedom, and Great Britain saw it differently. So, Britain sent the whole damn empire down on their heads. Australians, New Zealanders, Canadians, you name it. God, the Boers put up a fight, but we beat them in the end."

"I heard that you were a hero over there. That you won medals and everything."

"Francis, your father is a hero. A true Mountie. I'm just a man with a couple of medals stored in a cigar box, and I rarely look at the bloody things."

"He's being modest, Francis," Mike said.

Richard looked across the fire and locked eyes with Mike. The look in the constable's eyes told him that Mike wasn't mocking him now. Mike held a handful of snow against his bare arm; he had bruised it earlier loading up his sled. Richard could see the tattoo on Mike's right bicep — 2ND CANADIAN MOUNTED RIFLES. It reminded him of how long he and Mike had known each other. They certainly weren't friends while in Africa, but they served in the same unit. Though they had their troubles, that bond never truly broke.

Mike stopped staring and turned to Francis. "Did you know that Inspector Carol got shot over there, Francis? No kidding. He's leading a patrol one day. He's way up front and all the other men are many yards behind him, out of sight. The patrol is going through a rocky little valley and Inspector Carol comes upon a young Boer boy, maybe fourteen years old. The two of them start unloading their rifles at each other. The rest of the patrol hears the gunfire and comes running."

"What did they find?" Francis said.

Mike looked again at Richard with that same sombre expression in his eyes. "They see the Boer boy lying there with his life slipping away. And they see the Inspector kneeling next to the Boer boy, blood pouring out of the Inspector's pant leg, and he's trying to save the boy. The Inspector is wounded, and not doing anything to treat himself. He's too busy trying to help the boy. The rest of the men are shocked, but none of them stop the Inspector. They just pitch in."

"Did the boy live?"

Before answering, Mike puffed on his pipe and exhaled slowly. If Richard didn't know better, he would have thought Mike was doing it to add tension to his story.

Finally, he spoke. "Yeah, the boy lived. And the action was reported. Once his commanding officer learned about the Inspector's compassion to his enemy, even in the heat of battle, he recommended the inspector for a medal. Well, he didn't receive the medal *that time*. Our commanders felt that it would soften the fighting spirit of the men if he did. Instead, the inspector was mentioned in the dispatches. Pretty soon, though, every man in the regiment was talking about him."

Mike ended his story with a nod to Richard and Richard reciprocated. He wondered if this signalled a truce between Mike and him, at least for the remainder of this journey.

"God, what a tale!" Francis said. "Why haven't you written it down and sold it, Inspector?"

Mike tossed a handful of snow into Francis' face. "Not every man who fights in a war revels in it, Francis. In fact, most don't."

Francis was knocked into shame, and no one knew where to take the conversation after that. Richard rose from the fire to go relieve himself. As he walked past Francis, he patted his shoulder and said, "You can come over to my place sometime and take a look at my medals. And if you want, I'll tell you a couple of stories myself."

"Are you cold, Catherine?" Walter said as he pulled his wife close.

"Yes, freezing, but I know that it can get much colder. We'll be lucky if it doesn't drop to below forty degrees."

A crack rang out from between the trees, filling the night. Catherine flinched. "What was that?" she said.

Walter pulled her still closer, and she rested her head on his shoulder. "Relax, my love. It was just a branch breaking under the weight of the snow."

"I thought it might be something dangerous."

"Catherine, the animals won't bother us as long as we stay close to the fire, and there's no people within at least twenty miles of here."

"Are you sure?"

"Trust me," Walter said and kissed her cheek. "At this time of year, there's no one on the trail."

"Between the cold and the weird noises, I'm missing Kingston very much right now. Do you ever wish that we chose to stay there?" Catherine said.

"Sometimes I do," Walter said. "Sometimes I wonder why, for goodness sake, we ever moved up here." He gave Catherine a comforting smile. "But I don't want to be a baby about it."

Mike balked and leaned over the fire far enough that he almost singed himself. "What? You chose to come up here? I thought Francis was the only one of us silly enough to do that," he said. "Why in the devil did you do that?"

"We wanted a change of pace. Kingston's not the most buzzing city in Canada, but sometimes it felt a little too fast for us."

"Well, if slow is what you wanted, then you'll have plenty of it up here," Mike said.

Catherine smiled at Richard as he returned to the fire. "So, you never volunteered to come north, Richard?"

"No, senior command saw fit to transfer me here from Toronto, but I don't like thinking about it much either."

She didn't press him on the matter and instead looked over to Henry. He had been quiet since his dog had been shot. Ignoring the cold, he sat away from the fire and the warmth of the party's friendship. With his head lowered, he poked at the snow with a stick.

"Is he all right?" Catherine asked. "Henry looks so young to be out on the trail doing this sort of work."

Trapper turned to her but kept silent. It was clear that the old man wanted to speak, but Richard knew he wouldn't. That would be perceived as a father fighting his grown son's battles for him. What would the other men think of that?

"Henry's young but reliable," Walter said. "You remember last year when that group of trappers violated a woman in Fort McPherson and then fled south? Yeah, they had every Mountie out looking for them. Henry and a couple of Mounties found those trappers, and you bet that they put up a fight. Henry got a tooth punched out, but he gave a good account of himself. I heard he broke one man's nose. So, give a young man a chance to show you what he's made of."

Catherine nudged Walter in the ribs. "I thought I already had," she said and giggled.

She snuggled against her husband, and Richard could tell that it wasn't just for his heat.

Meanwhile, Francis had been watching his silent commanding officer for some time.

"Why are you so glum, Inspector?" Francis said.

Richard raised his head like he was waking from a daydream, surprised that someone was speaking to him. He hadn't realized that his mood showed.

"Oh, no great reason, Francis," Richard said. "I've never enjoyed this trail to begin with. And I'd rather be travelling it under better circumstances."

Mike held up his thermometer and casually waved it to get everyone's attention. "Minus thirteen degrees Fahrenheit everyone! Only minus thirteen? That's almost balmy for this time of year. Francis, go get your short pants, boy!"

Francis looked up from a snowshoe he had been checking for damage. The stunned look on his face sent the others over the edge, and they all howled with laughter.

The distraction made Francis bump one of the snowshoes into the fire. The end of the shoe lit before he scrambled to it and pulled it out. Richard cursed and moved over to examine the damage to the blackened top of the shoe.

"Foolish ass!" he cried. "Those snowshoes are your life!"

The scolding made Francis flinch, emphasizing the young constable's boyishness.

Following supper, everyone bedded down. Richard lay in his tent and thought about Catherine asking why Richard had ended up in the Yukon. It was part of Mountie folklore that the men posted to the Yukon were being punished. If you were caught accepting a bribe, or being insubordinate, or sleeping with the wife of a senior officer, then the service shipped you off to Canada's borderlands.

Richard never imagined that he would be among their numbers. His record of service was exemplary. He impressed senior command with his years of good conduct. On occasion, he even received some praise from his superiors.

However, it was his duty as a soldier in Africa that truly resonated with them. There, he had to serve in outposts and camps situated along a harsh frontier. The isolation that he faced demanded that he act at his own discretion, and he'd had to cope with what few resources were available. While the scorching winds of the African plains contrasted with the Yukon's bitter gales, it was easy to see similarities. His superiors believed that the Yukon needed proven men like him.

He remembered when they first told him that he was being sent to the Yukon. He only knew three things about it: The Yukon was big, hardly anyone lived there, and it was damned cold. All three points were confirmed with a quick check of a map and small talk with Mounties who had returned from there.

When he protested, his superintendent wrinkled his nose like he caught a whiff of manure. Richard was going. The decision had already been finalized.

His commanding officer said, "In this young century, Canada has a dire need to demonstrate its sovereignty. Between foreign fishing vessels, Arctic exploration, and the American military's ever-spreading hand, the Canadian north is too exposed. The need for a protective force, especially to the north and to the west, is very clear."

Richard hadn't disagreed with any of what his commanding officer had said. Much of the nation was still uncharted country, with Americans and other foreigners arriving only to establish their own microterritories within Canada. Richard heard too many stories of Americans flying their star-spangled banner on Canadian soil.

"Besides, what about frontier lawlessness? No one wants another Cypress Hills, Inspector," the superintendent added.

That was also true. No one wanted another Cypress Hills Massacre. A long time had passed since a group of American hunters crossed over the Canadian border from Montana and came into conflict with a camp of indigenous people, the Assiniboine. Gunfire and chaos resulted in the deaths of twenty-four people, almost all Assiniboine. Some were women and children. The Mounties still referenced the slaughter, but they never wanted to speak about it or remember it in detail. Once in a while, a Mountie was inclined to say, "No one wants another Cypress Hills."

Canadians were outraged by Cypress Hills, and the terrible episode reinforced the government's existing plans to build a new, protective police service.

It was clear to Prime Minister MacDonald what was needed. Armed men of authority to range across the open land and protect the freedom of this young nation. Its members would wear a redcoat, called the Red Serge, following the tradition of the old British redcoat soldiers. Those soldiers had garnered trust, respect, and acclaim among the indigenous people, so if Canadian police dressed the same, would they not gain some of the same credibility?

The first Mounties, the North West Mounted Police, were created the same year as the massacre, in 1873, to keep sovereignty and uphold the law across Canada's great expanse.

Richard's commanding officer gave him a smile of reassurance.

"Besides, how difficult could it be, Inspector? A large part of the job will be simple patrolling. You will set out by horse or dogsled, looking for safety hazards or assisting people in distress. That doesn't sound too rough for a city Mountie like you."

A friend in the service who had served in the Yukon prior was quick to correct this assessment.

"Richard, the Yukon isn't the big city, and big city policing doesn't work there. That is some real frontier living, Richie. You'll need more than a solid billy club and a whistle to keep the peace up there, boy."

He had been right. The Yukon tested even Richard's pioneering skills, and Richard was no stranger to roughing it. His time in the army had seen to that.

For three years, he had been stuck at Fort MacCammon. He knew that his superintendent was unimpressed with him. It was a wonder that Richard had been left in charge of the fort. He was suspicious that that senior command wanted Fort MacCammon to fail. They just needed a scapegoat to blame it on afterwards.

Several times, Richard thought about leaving the service. Many Mounties chose to give up life as lawmen to become entrepreneurs in a Yukon that was teeming with opportunity. The diverse work experience of the Mounties meant that they were likely the best suited people for the north's labour market. Most of the Mounties who left the service became public bureaucrats, trail guides, businessmen, and anything else they wanted to be.

Some even became prospectors. Who could blame them? Mountie wages were low. How long could any of them keep arresting drunken, ill-bred louts who had more money in their pockets than the lawmen had in the bank?

During the Gold Rush, Richard knew of two men who had left the service together to become gold prospectors. They had asked Richard to join them.

"You would have a better chance of finding gold at the end of a rainbow. It wouldn't be so cold either!" he told them.

In retrospect, he could have said something nicer — maybe even wished them luck. Either way, the joke was on Richard. The pair hit pay dirt just outside of Dawson, and both now lived like kings in the United States.

Richard sulked and rolled over in his sleeping bag. He was an inspector now, and there were few positions above his rank that ever became available. And in the north, you had to be touched by the hand of God to get one. He was certain that he would finish his career as he was now: an officer without distinction, patrolling the edge of the British Empire. With that sadness, Richard finally drifted off.

Chapter 8

The next day came, and the patrol made its way down a hill slope passing through rows of pine. Its grade wasn't steep, so it favoured the dogsleds. The dogs were pulling quickly now, doing an excellent job of beating down the trail. The party's members jogged behind the sleds. To his right, Richard could see rabbit prints leading off the trial and into the trees. The prints of a stalking fox mingled with them. He chuckled. Richard had no reason to care for either the rabbit or the fox, but regardless, he wished the rabbit good luck.

The morning was turning out to be easier than he expected. His was now the lead sled, and he could see that the trail ahead was clear of deadfall. The snowfall had kept up through the night, but it was so light that he wasn't concerned.

The only bother was the debate during lunch and the tension it had caused.

Over his coffee, Mike said, "The way I see it, the Mounties have two jobs to do in the north. We need to protect the borders from the Russians, Americans, and everybody else who wants to stick a flag in it, and we have to give some law and order to this land."

Walter said, "You're right about that, Mike. I remember when the North West Mounted Police first spread to the Yukon. I was one of the first Mounties to come up here. It was just before the Gold Rush began, and, with it, came an awful need for police. Too many outlanders arrived, hungry for gold."

Walter grimaced and looked away from the trail, as if there was something dirty in front of him.

"Why, almost all of them ended up robbed, lost, or dead. And here we Mounties were in the middle of it all. Since we were some of the only people with authority in the territories, we had to do all sorts of things: delivering the mail, collecting duties, customs activities, wildlife research, land surveying, and even doctoring sometimes."

"We still do those things!" Mike said.

"Yeah, but not to the same scale. I had to deliver more than one baby, I can tell you!" Walter said.

Catherine shot him a look and he quickly added, "I had a little help from my wife, of course."

Mike saw Walter was on his side, so he continued with his argument.

"The lawlessness of the north couldn't last forever," Mike said. "What? Miners making up their own rules, saying who could do what, executing people!"

Trapper stared expressionlessly at these words. "And what about the part where you take money from everybody coming in and out of this land? Is that part of protecting freedoms or upholding justice?"

Richard knew that Trapper was right. The Mounties collected a great sum of revenue for Ottawa through duties, license, and taxes.

Mike continued, "Well, things like law and governance don't pay for themselves, Trapper. Money needs to be collected to cover the cost. I would've thought a smart man like you would know that already."

Trapper frowned. "This land only became lawless once the white man came. There was another code, an older code, one that they spoiled."

The contempt in the old man's voice was unmistakable.

"The bottom line is that the north needed the police. That sort of loose justice didn't do anyone any favours, especially for your people," Mike said.

"And what justice is that, Constable? The one where our men are tried for charges they may not understand? Where they receive a trial in a language that is unclear to them?"

"I know that the Mountie is a living symbol of justice and Canadian sovereignty," Mike said.

Richard heard the conviction in Mike's voice and knew that Mike believed this statement would bring an end to the debate.

"Mike, I have seen relations between the police and my people strained for decades. Every year, more and more white people came to the territories to settle, make money, chart the land, or spread the word of God. The landscape is dotted with the white man's forts, trappers' cabins, work camps, whaling stations, and trading posts of your all- powerful Hudson's Bay Company. No matter what their intentions, they press upon the land of my people. They hunt the game, spread disease, and, perhaps worst of all, spread alcohol. You know the booze sold by the whites to us is nothing but mixed tobacco juice, strychnine, and God knows what else. It does nothing for us but give skull-busting headaches and gut-rot. If the booze doesn't kill us, we are wishing that it did."

"Hey, no one forces it to your lips," Mike said, shrugging his shoulders. "What do you think of this matter, Inspector?"

Both Mike and Trapper looked to him, and Richard knew that the two men were waiting for him to end this argument. Because he was the party's leader, his opinion was not only his opinion — it was the final say. Richard wanted to give due care before answering.

He knew the history of law and order in the north very well. His lonely evenings next to a bookcase gave him ample time to learn about the relationship between the Crown's representatives and the indigenous people. From the Alaska-Yukon border east to Hudson's Bay, relations between the two groups were agreeable. At least, this was how he saw them. The two traded together, lived together, and built together. If not, then how could anyone explain the mixed marriages that were becoming more common in the territories?

Certainly, there was some hostility on occasion. Tension and aggression existed since Sir Martin Frobisher led his expedition from England in the late sixteenth century. This was sometimes caused by the white man's undue violence and exploitation. It grieved him to admit that, but that was the reality. On occasion, that provoked a violent response from the original people of this land.

Of course, not all the fighting was over the territory and its wealth. As Trapper said, the people of the north had their own governmental framework before the whites arrived. They had their own rules, formal processes, and hierarchy. There were bound to be conflicts. The displacement of this structure by that of the whites was, Richard thought, almost inevitable. And as Mike noted, miners themselves were setting up their own systems of laws. As if the matter needed to be complicated any further.

Finally, Richard said, "I think that we are all God's children, Constable. And, if this is true, then every man is my brother, and I should treat my brothers as I would want and expect my brothers to treat me."

Trapper smiled at these words. This made Richard swell with guilt. He did feel a partnership, and even fraternity, with Trapper. But his faith in God had declined these last few years. Using Christianity now seemed so hollow.

Then again, he told himself, what better use of that religion than to settle an argument?

In any case, Richard wasn't about to have the good will demonstrated thus far in the journey ruined by grievances that were beyond any of their control.

"Enough with the history lessons, both of you," he said. "We have a lot of work to do together without adding to the burden."

***

Two hours had passed, and now they were again travelling in silence. Richard was hoping that the quiet would help his debaters to settle when he saw a bridge ahead. A second bridge lay only two hundred feet beyond it, in plain sight.

He stopped his sled next to the first bridge and called for the party to halt. During his first Winter Patrol, Richard learned its name — Rusty Bridge. He had joked about its safety to the other men, but that only made him look like a novice. Standing in front of the crossing, he saw how sturdy it was. Though a layer of snow covered the bridge, Richard knew small boards lay on top, parallel to the logs and nailed into place. Even without these boards fastening the logs together, the cold had surely frozen the logs to each other.

He looked over the ravine's edge. If it had been spring, he would have heard the bubbling little stream that runs through there and seen the ravine's vertical, red walls that gave the bridge its name running down to the stony bottom seventy feet below. But it was December, so all he saw was snow rising from the ravine's floor to meet him and the snow-caked walls that looked to be shedding their rock.

"Well, the bridge looks sturdy enough to carry a couple of sleds at once, but I still want one sled crossing at a time. If any dogs get scared out there, I want only one man on that crossing."

"I'll go first," Henry said. His father shot him a look that said his son had spoken when he should not have.

"No, that's fine. I'll go," Richard responded. He was mindful of his position as the party's leader.

Richard walked behind the sled as he crossed, taking baby steps the whole way.

He shouted at his dogs, which seemed unaware of the hazard that lay under their paws. His arms strained to control the sled's balance. Though the bridge only took seconds to cross, if the sled tipped over the sides, it would pull the whole dog team with it. When he reached the other side, he looked back at the men. He could see their confidence had risen.

"That was easy enough," he called to them.

Mike stared at the sky. "The snow is getting heavier now, Inspector. Shouldn't we stop and make camp?"

"We'll break once we've cleared the next bridge. I don't want to try manoeuvring the dogs and sleds over that after it has been buried under another couple of inches."

As soon as the others had crossed, they continued the two hundred feet to the next bridge. Richard again stopped his sled and called halt. He saw two of his dogs lift their heads and turn them to the left in unison. Richard knew the importance of trusting a dog's snout and fine ears while travelling in the wilderness. He surveyed the landscape leftwards: trees, trees, and of course, this second ravine's craggy cliffs.

"It's just a rabbit," Trapper murmured. Richard smiled at that. Of course the old man was reading the dogs as Richard was.

"I'll go first this time, with your permission, Inspector," Trapper said.

"Thank you, sir. Please, when you are ready," Richard replied.

Trapper drove his sled towards the bridge. Across the ravine, Richard could make out a rabbit's head poking out from behind a birch. "Roast rabbit for supper, Trapper?" he called.

"Sounds g— "

Trapper's words were cut short by a sharp crack. It was most certainly a gunshot. Its report hung in the air the way all gunshots in the wilderness do. Trapper seized up and lurched forward, looking like he suddenly needed to move his bowels. Richard heard Trapper breathe out, and that exhale turned into a rasp.

The forest exploded. The gunfire now came as a symphony. The crack of rifles was punctuated by roaring shotgun blasts. The soft crash of the lower-powered pistols seemed distant. Trapper's body jigged and spasmed with each hit. His head lifted and wrenched as if it wanted to get away from his neck. Richard saw Trapper's head snap back so quickly that he knew the old man was dead. The heads of living men just don't swing that way. Trapper finally fell, but, by then, he was gone from this world.

The sled dogs swarmed around Richard, thrashing their heads and prancing. Their harness straps caught his legs and pulled him to the ground. At least, while under their cover, it gave Richard a few merciful moments in which he was no longer in the line of fire. Some dogs took bullets, yelping, barking, and falling into the snow alongside him.

Old soldier's instincts took over. Richard crawled behind his sled to hide from the attackers' sight. He did not need dogs' ears now to know that the attackers lay to the right. From the direction of the gunfire, it sounded like they were on the same side of the bridge as Richard and the rest of his party. He looked around the side of his sled and scanned the land. He saw no one. Richard cursed the trees. They cast too many shadows. The few grey slivers of sunlight gave no aid.

He guessed at the number of attackers. There were many, at least five of them. He could make out small puffs of smoke and muzzle flashes rising from a heap of pines less than three hundred feet from the party. The patrol, his patrol, had walked into the jaws of a well-laid trap.

Richard couldn't see anyone in the woods on the opposite side of the ravine. If he could get across the bridge, he could be clear of the ambush. He looked back to the party and saw Mike had pulled his pistol from its holster. He aimed at the trees and pulled the trigger. Nothing happened. The intense cold had frozen the gun's metal parts together. That intricate assembly of cylinder, action, trigger, and barrel might just as well have been a block of ice. It was an amateur's mistake. How could Mike have let his sidearm freeze?

Walter lay on the ground. He looked skywards and his hand lay across his chest. *He's as good as dead*, Richard thought. Catherine cried out and ran to her husband, and Mike dove to catch her about the waist. Walter had become a bull's eye, with bullets kicking up snow around him.

Snow dusted across his face, and Richard could not tell if the man was still conscious.

The other men had gotten their weapons into action, even if they aimed only at the wilderness. Richard grabbed his Winchester from the sled. On his belly, he tried to work the rifle's lever action. No good. The action kept catching in the snow and fouling the gun's whole operation. What he wouldn't give for a good, bolt-action gun.

"We need to move! We're done for if we stay out here!" Mike called.

At least, Richard thought it was Mike. It was difficult to tell over the din of fire. He pushed the gun aside and crawled through the obstacle course of dog's legs and overturned sleds.

The world started to decelerate, like slow-moving frames in a picture show. With each frame, Richard spotted everything in perfect clarity, but his brain raced to catch up with what he saw. He stood and lunged towards the bridge — his salvation. The gun smoke's acridity punched him in the nose. It was so thick that it bit his eyes, and his throat dried. Choking, eyes watering, Richard waved his arms before him.

His vision blurred. Light-headedness came immediately after.

Oh God, he thought, don't pass out!

His heart was pushing the rest of his chest outwards. Then his chest tightened, and Richard wanted to vomit. Panic was going to get him killed, he was sure of it. He was losing his nerve right there on that lousy little, God-forsaken trail. After a lifetime of close calls, death was finally upon him.

Everything was moving even slower now — a nightmare where a monster was chasing him, but he was running at a fraction of the needed speed. A bullet struck a large rock eight feet from his left side. The ricochet's alien whine scared him as badly as the gunfire. A second bullet hit the same rock, and that sound repeated. He was being targeted. Any moment, his head would fill the sights of a gunman's rifle, and that head would wrench on his neck, just like Trapper's did. Richard willed his feet to move faster, but they were too slow. Everything was … too … damn … slow!

Richard saw Mike and Catherine before him. They had piled onto his sled. Mike manoeuvred it past the others and to the front of the bridge. His dogs did not hesitate to move forward on the crossing, and Mike handled them well. Richard almost cheered when the two of them made it across.

Richard was halfway across the bridge by the time they had crossed. Ahead of him, he saw stray rounds blowing off the bridge's tree bark. Behind him, Henry and Francis jockeyed against each other to be the next across. Both men were driving their sleds ahead of them. At least, they were trying to.

"Leave the damn sleds! Just run! Run!" Richard cried as he finally crossed to the ravine's other side. But panic had overtaken them. The two men kept pushing forward and against each other. Some of the dogs they drove before them were already dead. Their bodies were trampled and ground-up by their teammates and the sleds' skids.

Then, Richard heard a sickening crack that was much louder than any of the gunshots. Richard looked to the bridge's logs and opened his mouth to curse. Too late — it only took half a second for the bridge to fold like a book. Some dogs yelped as the broken logs fell against them. Henry managed one cry that sounded more like shock than pain. Sleds, men, dogs, and logs tumbled downwards all together.

Francis and Henry are dead, Richard thought. If they weren't killed just now, they will die soon.

In the heat of the moment, one of the attackers grew bold and emerged from the darkness. He was a full head taller than Richard, and his fur coat made his shoulders look impossibly broad. The ogre charged for the ravine, firing his rifle. Richard could see the ecstasy on the man's face while he unloaded. Battle rage had seized the man, and now he was running in for the killing blow. Richard saw his chance and took it.

Richard tore off his mitts and fumbled under his coat. Precious seconds lost. While reaching for his pistol, Richard sized up the shot. The man was now a hundred feet from him — a hard shot, even for a good marksman. The man was too far away. There wasn't enough time to aim. The whole moment was too hot.

His hand finally snatched his pistol. He whipped his arm towards the ogre so quickly that the man may have thought Richard was throwing the pistol at him. Richard was about to pull the trigger but paused. Instead of pulling the trigger, he first cocked the hammer. It meant that less pull on the trigger was now needed to fire a round. Less pull on the trigger meant a steadier hand, which meant a more precise shot. With the trigger already drawn back, Richard gave the trigger no more than a gentle press.

The Colt erupted. It launched its .455 slug, which crashed into the man's face. The bulky pistol's report was surprisingly loud, like a little rifle shot rather than one from a pistol. The heavy recoil cracked Richard's wrist backwards so badly that he thought it was sprained. A tingling shot up his arm, and it was a wonder that he managed to hold on to the big gun. But the bullet had done its job. A hole the size of a chess piece had burst open where the big man's right cheekbone used to be. He made no sound as he fell back, away from the inspector, his face a bloody wreck. All the while, Richard slipped towards a tangle of underbrush. He was grateful to have fired his weapon at least once.

Richard knew that escape was his only option now — his only hope. He turned his back on the horror scene and ran. From the ravine behind him, Richard heard the whimpering of what he hoped were dying dogs.

Chapter 9

The ambushers stood beside the ravine's edge. Below them lay a twist of wood and pounded meat. Yelping came from that pile. No one in Azarov's party could say if the sounds were made by men or dogs.

"How the hell do we get down to them?" said Lottery.

"We don't," Azarov said. "We want them dead, and they are working on that now."

The ambush went worse than expected. He and his men had sabotaged the bridge by cutting its logs and letting the falling snow cover their tracks and handiwork. They had hoped to kill or trap all of their prey, but some had escaped across the now-broken bridge before its collapse. Even worse, Azarov's party was now trapped on the ravine's opposite side.

He sighed, and looked on the bright side. He and his men had been blessed with a snowfall. As well, they had kept their own dogs out of sight and quiet long enough to draw the Mounties into an ambush. When he saw some of the Mounties' dogs turning and barking, Azarov thought for certain that his party would be detected, but they hadn't been. What's more, only one of his men had been killed in the shooting.

Azarov watched Lang and wondered if the corrupt Mountie knew any of the police that he just helped to ambush.

When asked, Lang said, "That's Walter Sands over there. I worked with him a couple of times, but that's it." Lang gestured to Trapper's shredded body. "That one over there, I met him but never bothered to learn his name. And God knows who is down there at the bottom of that mess."

Lang leaned over the ravine's edge, apparently looking for a familiar face. "I never really got a look at any of the ones who got away. Except for Richard Carol. He must be their leader."

"Inspector Richard Carol?" Azarov said.

"Oh, you know him?"

"I met him once. Not very impressive. If he is their leader, then we won't have any trouble finishing this now."

Lang snorted. Azarov wondered if he meant anything by it, or if he only wanted to annoy Azarov. He watched Lang to give an indication, but there was none. Lang only kept peering into the ravine. He felt his disgust for Lang tremble outwards from his core and into his hands, and he had the sudden urge to push the man and add him to the pile of bodies below. Azarov had heard stories about Lang from other corrupt Mounties. Apparently, Lang had disgraced himself with some unspeakable poor conduct in British Columbia and was sent to the Yukon as a punishment. If it were not for his family's high status and charitable donations in the west, he would have been thrown out of the service.

Azarov turned his attention away from Lang and looked across the ravine. The heavy snow was blanketing the tree branches, making it difficult to see through the woods. The white branches flared red with specks of blood. The Mounties were bleeding.

"They're hurt," Lottery said.

"Yes, but we could not have hurt them too badly. They are still able to run. Don't be bold, Lottery."

Their prey had already fled deep into the trail. Azarov raised his head and saw that the sky had churned charcoal. The wind was worsening. He knew what that meant. Many years at sea taught him how to predict the weather.

"A storm is coming," Azarov said. Snow brushed across his eyes, stressing his point. "We must end this now — the quicker, the better. Get back to the sleds. We are leaving in ten minutes."

"For where?" Lang asked.

It was Lottery who answered, quick to sense that his boss wasn't in the mood for questions.

"There is another bridge, a smaller one, about five miles down the ravine. We can cross there and follow the ravine's edge back up here to the trail."

Lottery then looked at Azarov. "It will take some time."

Azarov's reply was simple. "And to think, you only have nine minutes now."

"Boss, that other bridge is too narrow and weak for sleds. It would never take their weight. We'll have to cross on foot."

"We will leave the dogs and sleds behind after we get there."

"Can't we unharness the dogs and use them to hunt?" Lang asked.

Azarov scowled. "Do they look like trained bloodhounds to you? They don't know how to scent hunt!"

"He's right," Lottery chimed in. "In the harness, the sled dogs are as good as steam engines. Out of the harness, they are just a pack of half-wild mutts."

He pointed to the group of dogs. They were already pawing and sniffing at the corpses.

"Even if you could get them to follow the police, how long do you think it would be before they started chasing after the scent of the nearest rabbit?"

"What are the dogs going to eat?" Lang said. "Maybe we should cut our losses and head for home."

"Worry about what you will eat," Azarov snorted. He knew that this bullshit was coming, and he had already scripted his response. "Lang, what do you think will happen if word gets out about what we have done already? We killed a Mountie posse. The Mounted Police will hunt us across the British Empire. When they catch us, we can look forward to our last days inside cold prison rooms, eating colder food, before they finally hang us. No judge would grant any of us so much as a handful of leniency."

Lang and the others looked away from him. There was no arguing with his points. They had already crossed a line and travelled into a new country from which they could not leave.

"Now, get yourselves together. We leave now."

As the group broke apart, Azarov grabbed Lang's shoulder.

Azarov said, "Weasel, this isn't the first time in this trip that I have cursed myself for bringing you along. I only let you come because Morgan pushed you onto me. But, if you keep disrespecting me, I'll leave you out here too."

Lang glared at him. "Don't call me that," he said. "I'm a Mountie. You will show some respect."

"You? A Mountie? Don't make me laugh. Just because you wear the uniform, that doesn't make you a Mountie. You are one of Morgan's dogs, just like the rest of us, and worse than some of us. Other men here do what they do because they have no other choice for paying work. You have a job, but you are just greedy. I know what Morgan pays you, Weasel."

Lang looked down at Azarov with his beady eyes. "When we get back to Dawson, you and I are going to have a talk with Morgan. He's going to hear all about what happened on the trail, including your failures in leadership."

Azarov thought of his wife and daughters, as well as their forthcoming journey away from Dawson, away from Morgan.

"Leadership?" Azarov said. "You're welcome to it."

***

Richard pushed himself down the trail. He felt his leg cramping and thought, *Don't seize up on me, damn it. Not now.* He felt the coating of sweat all over him. His panting flooded his lungs with the frosted air. After a few breaths, his lungs started to hurt, so he began to take in his air through pursed lips.

At least the trail was, by and large, beaten down already. When he looked carefully enough, he could make out some of the partly-covered old tracks of his attackers. Much of the trail's snow had been pressed into the ground, and fallen trees had been cleared. Now, he escaped his enemies in their own footsteps. They must have travelled towards Fort MacCammon on this same trail only a day or so before.

Still, Richard could not believe his misfortune. Most of the party was now dead. This included Trapper, who he had believed was his greatest resource on this journey. The only two surviving members that he knew of lay ahead of him. He called for Mike and Catherine to stop. They kept going, with Catherine staggering under Mike's weight. He was using her as a human crutch. Richard called for Mike and Catherine to stop four more times before they did. They were as wild with fear as he was.

When he caught up with them, he was so dizzy that he almost fell over. There wasn't enough blood or air or anything else reaching his brain. He placed a hand on his hammering heart.

Catherine rushed to hug Richard. "Walter is dead!" she cried. "I saw him. He's dead!"

Richard grabbed her by the shoulders and pulled her close. "I know. He's gone. I'm so sorry, Catherine. They're all gone. Are you both all right?"

"I'm fine, but Mike has been shot in the belly. I better take a look at him and at that arm," Catherine said, pointing at Richard.

He followed her stare to his left arm. He hadn't even noticed that a bullet had sliced through his coat and grazed his skin. Blood drops dotted the snow behind him.

He could tell that Mike's wound was far worse. The constable was crumpled in a snowdrift with his knees drawn up close to his chest. Richard pulled Mike to his feet with Catherine's help. Even working as a pair, they struggled to lift him.

The twisting of his torn insides made Mike cry out in agony.

"It's burning! It's burning!" he cried, until his cries ceased to sound like the cries of a man, and he made only a yapping.

"Come on, Mike. We have to keep going. If we stop, we'll freeze," Richard said.

The reality was that Mike was already freezing. His skin was gray and his forehead clammy. His teeth chattered, and his whole body shuddered violently. So much of his hot blood had emptied out onto the snow.

"He won't last long out here," Richard said to Catherine. "He's losing too much blood. He'll be dead in an hour. We're less than a mile away from a cabin built as a temporary lodging for Mounties. There, we can treat him, get shelter, and resupply.

Catherine conceded to this without a word. Even to someone in a state of shock, shelter would sound like a good idea under these circumstances. She placed herself under Mike's shoulder.

"What about those people who shot at us?" she asked.

"That was a mistake," she continued. Richard could hear her choking back the sobs. "That was a police party, like us, tracking after Azarov just like we are. Don't you see? They thought we were Azarov and his men, and they opened fire."

"Catherine, that *was* Azarov's group. Those men shot to kill. They never gave a warning. No chance to surrender. Mounties never would have done that, not even when hunting scoundrels like Azarov."

"No, you're wrong, Richard. It was an accident. A terrible accident."

"It was no accident! It was a slaughter!" he yelled.

Richard hated to raise his voice, but he had seen her condition many times before. He had seen people in devastating situations trying to make sense of it all. Trying to reshape it in their minds to be something less catastrophic or evil. It was a defensive wall that humans erected to shield themselves when reality became too frightening.

Richard, said, "Look Catherine, I'm so sorry, but we don't have time for all of this. Just take my word for it that it was Azarov, that same bastard who shot the reverend and his own men. I'm certain of it. We've underestimated our enemies, my dear. They're far more ruthless and brazen than we imagined. We paid a steep price for it today. Some of us paid more than others, but we're going to get out of this. I promise. Now come on. We need to get some shelter fast."

She nodded to Richard and pressed a piece of cloth against Mike's torn abdomen.

Richard continued. "There's another bridge, a smaller one, quite a journey from here. They'll cross there and rejoin the trail. Then, they'll run us down."

"Perhaps they'll leave us alone. Maybe they'll run away."

"Not bloody likely, and if you're thinking someone might come along to help us, you can forget that too. The trail is quiet at this time of year. Besides, if those men would attack a Mountie patrol, then who would they fear? Certainly not some fur trappers checking their trap lines."

Seeing the worry on her face, he added, "I don't know this area well, but I'm sure that those men know it even less. Maybe we can use that to our advantage. It will be all right, Catherine. We're going to get out of this, we just don't know how yet."

Her expression never changed. Richard couldn't blame her for that. Lately, everything he said sounded false.

***

They hadn't travelled far before their sanctuary came into sight — the cabin. An abandoned sawmill sat next to this shack. When Richard first saw the cabin years earlier, he assumed this site had been chosen because the sawmill's close proximity meant easy firewood. However, the mill's sole saw blade, browning with rust, told him otherwise. It hadn't been used in years. The remains of its final victims lay as heaps of rotting sawdust near its sides. Some of the mill's boards had been torn away and used to quicken the construction of the cabin. As a consequence, the cabin was a patchwork of well-cut planks and rough logs, all chinked with moss for insulation.

By the time they reached the cabin, Richard was sweating but very cold. The ache in his chest was a throb now. If he hadn't stopped smoking years ago, he would already be dead.

He stepped through the cabin doorway, and he felt heat strike his face.

That isn't heat, he thought. It is just less cold in here than out there.

The one-room cabin was still fairly new — perhaps only ten years old. It was three feet above the ground. Like so many other buildings, the cabin sat on stilts to protect it from snow and water damage. Its roof bowed downwards under the weight of so many past snowfalls.

He handed his police notebook to Catherine, knowing it would best serve them now for lighting a fire.

"We need to get heat in here. Fast!" Richard said.

Taking her cue, Catherine got to work building a fire at the cabin's stove. The cold and her eagerness made her clumsy. She fumbled with the matches left on the stovetop. It took her three tries before she lit the paper.

Meanwhile, Richard assisted Mike to the cabin's only bunk. He looked underneath Mike's two coats and shirt. The bullet hole was tiny, and an inch left of his navel, but his belly was slick with the sort of dark blood that is seen only with critical injuries. When he circled his hand around to Mike's back, Richard didn't feel an exit wound. He knew better than to remove the bullet. The best thing he could do was try to cover the wound to slow blood loss.

"It isn't that bad, Mike," Richard lied. He touched the constable's shoulder. "I'm not surprised that you shot your way through the trap. Ambushes were as common as guard duty in Africa, yes?"

"I still took a hit, didn't I?"

"And did you hit any of them, Constable? Please tell me that you did."

"No, sir. I'm quite certain that I missed every shot. I don't think Henry or Francis got a shot off before they went ass over applecart into that ravine. I am damn sure that Trapper didn't."

"And Walter?"

"Let's not speak of him for now," Mike said and glanced towards Catherine at the stove. "What about you? Did you shoot anything?"

"I got one. Hit him more so by good luck than good marksmanship. I can guarantee that."

Mike winced with pain and held his belly. "Damn us for not seeing that ambush, Inspector. It was the sort of skulking warfare that we both saw in Africa. If those men had been better trained, we would both surely be dead now."

Richard frowned and wondered if they had only delayed their demise. He knew that their chances of survival were middling. Assuming that they were not run down like frightened rabbits, they would be killed by the cold, starvation, or exhaustion. He knew that Mike was thinking the same.

"What happened back there was my fault, Constable. I played the cards wrong and walked all of you into that trap. Where was my intuition when I needed it?"

"You can't blame yourself, Richard. That trap was well laid. The ambushers could have hit us at the first bridge, but chose to do otherwise. They let us cross the first bridge to give us a feeling of security, only to attack at the second. Whoever planned that attack has played this game before, I'm sure of it. And how could you have known that they would have been so brazen as to ambush a Mountie patrol? I certainly wouldn't have played my cards any better. Inspector, you aren't to blame for any of this."

"Here's the real problem, Constable. How do we shake them off our tails when they don't have anywhere else to go but stay on the same trail as us?"

Mike flinched with pain as he tried to roll onto his side. Richard placed a hand on Mike's shoulder and pulled him over. After he caught a breath, a smile touched Mike's lips. "I've devoted some thought to that already. The observatory. We can run for the observatory. We can slip off the trail, down the side path to the observatory. They already tore up the trail on their way from Dawson, with at least half a dozen dogsleds and the prints left by dozens of dogs and men. Surely, it would be difficult to tell our new tracks form their old ones, especially at night. Hell, they might chase old tracks for miles before they realize that we gave them the slip."

Richard chewed his lower lip. Reaching the observatory would put them in a much better position. It meant shelter, and its position on a hilltop gave the high-ground advantage.

"But they'll see our tracks leading off the main trail to the side trail," Richard said.

Mike shrugged. "We can do our best to cover our tracks at the juncture where the main trail and the path to the observatory meet. Then, pray that they are so set on following the main trail that they pass by. We can even remove the sign at the juncture to the observatory, so they'll think it's farther down the trail."

Richard turned this over in his mind. Could their pursuers be fooled into walking past this side path? It wasn't a perfect plan, but it wasn't a bad one either. More importantly, it was the only plan that they had for the moment.

Richard felt guilt pinching him. He was supposed to be leading the patrol. Now, most of it was dead, and his subordinate was the one arranging their escape. Then, admiration swept away his guilt. The smarmy constable whom he was always battling had survived an ambush and was showing his resourcefulness.

"All right," Richard said. "Let's do it."

Mike's smile filled Richard with hope.

"Rest now, Mike. Catherine will take a look at you in a moment. I better take inventory."

Richard turned away. He reached for his gunbelt and counted how many rounds he had. In the right corner of the cabin were three wooden crates, each marked SUPPLIES — PROPERTY OF NORTH WEST MOUNTED POLICE. The service had not gone by that name since 1904, so Richard knew that their contents were at least a few years old.

He opened one crate. It included a cloth pack, which was helpful, since Richard had fled the ambush without his own. He also found a small hand axe. He rubbed his thumb across its blade. He couldn't have asked for any sharper. Richard tucked the hatchet into his pack.

"Thank God," Mike said from his bunk. "If you are in the woods, and you have only one tool, let it be an axe." The cabin's low light caught something flashing at the bottom of the crate. Richard pulled out a metal flask, opened it, and sniffed its cap. Rum. Not a bad thing to have if you're a cold Mountie in the woods. He put it into the pack and hoped that the others didn't see. Before this fight was finished, he had a feeling that he would need it. Any reservations he had about alcohol were quickly flying out the cabin's window.

In the north, it was a ritual to place at least one rifle in any cache of supplies. These were the next things Richard reached for. It was clear that whoever had loaded these kits had included guns that they wanted to get rid of.

Of the two guns, the first was a Snider–Enfield rifle, long and elegantly crafted. He held it in his hands and studied its condition. It was a single-shot, breech-loading rifle that Richard had never used before, or, if he had, he could not remember it now. The Snider–Enfield had been abandoned by the Mounties over twenty years earlier.

"Now's not the time to learn a new gun," he muttered. He discarded it, feeling it would be of little use against his enemies.

His heart sank when he examined the next rifle. It was a lever-action Winchester Model 1894 with a cracked stock and spots of rust on the lever. He could only imagine what the bore of the rifle looked like. He thought he was likely to kill himself with this piece of rubbish, assuming it could fire at all. He thought about the heartless devil who left this rifle here in such poor shape, and wished he had that man's name and address. Grudgingly, he slung it over his shoulder.

The next firearm was a six-shot revolver, an Enfield Mk II. Now here was a weapon that Richard knew well. It was a predecessor to the currently issued Colt. Like many Mounties, Richard felt that the Enfield was too heavy and bulky for long patrols. It was a pig of a gun. Ugly, unreliable, and lacking power. It would have to do. Richard wondered how well he could shoot with a gun in which he had no faith.

"Well, more guns right now certainly wouldn't hurt," he murmured to himself.

He gave the cabin a check to see if there was anything else of value. On the cabin's table was a leather-bound logbook and a pencil set. The cabin's planners had the good sense to keep a record of who used the cabin, when, and any other worthwhile details.

He lit the table's oil lamp and studied the book, thumbing through the pages.

"How can I use this?" he whispered.

He could scribble his last will and testament. He could give descriptions of what was likely to be his future murderers. At least that gave a better chance of justice being served after his death. If only the cabin was used more. Then, the logbook could be used to leave a message for help. But what good would that do him when the last entry was logged over a year ago?

An answer took shape. Richard was surprised by the speed at which his plan formed. He never needed to signal for help. He only needed to make it look like he was signalling for help. He took the pencil and began to write.

Dec. 15, 1907

Help! My three companions have been murdered by a gang of bandits who have effectively taken control of Dawson City. While travelling from Fort MacCammon to Dawson to take control of the city, we were attacked by these men who were determined to stop any legal authorities from reaching Dawson. These murderers are now hunting us, thus, we are now heading directly for Dawson, and as quickly as possible. Please give any aid that you can without delay.

In God's Hands,

Inspector Richard Carol

He reviewed his log entry and frowned. It was brief, choppy, and inelegant. Nonetheless, it included the main points, but he didn't have the luxury of time. He hoped that his new enemies would fall for his trick. If he could set it in their minds that he and his companions were heading straight for Dawson, when really they had slipped down a side trail to the observatory, they might yet survive.

He left the logbook open and in plain view on the table. Surely, their pursuers would find it.

He was anxious to get moving again, but he knew they needed to warm themselves. So, he took the pencil and some empty pages from the notebook and walked over the stove. Richard used a moment to warm his hands by the fire. Rubbing his hands together, he wished that he still had his mitts. Then, he scribbled onto the pages.

"What are you writing?" Catherine asked while she tended to Mike.

"A detailed description of what happened and who did it. If we don't survive this, then at least there will be a written record of what occurred."

Catherine nodded. "Good idea. I remember once reading about a police officer who had been shot. Before he died, he wrote down a description of his murderer in his police notebook. When his body was found, his notes were read, and the murderer was arrested."

"Yes, I think they taught that same police folktale to us when we were in training. How are you holding up, Catherine?"

It was a stupid question to ask. Tears blurred her eyes while she finished dressing Mike's wound. The image of her husband being killed was obviously fresh in her mind. Richard recalled how he felt when Rose passed away, only Walter did not pass away. He was cut down without warning or provocation.

"I know you're hurting so badly right now. I wish I could take it all away. But I want you to know that we're going to get out of this, Catherine. We have a plan. We are going to make a run for the observatory."

She sniffed and said, "What's that?"

"The observatory is like a laboratory and a house, all-in-one. It was built to shelter and support the work of British scientists who are studying the Yukon. It's small — separated into two rooms, living quarters for its inhabitants and a workspace. The latter is filled with all manner of instruments … barometers, thermometers, compasses, and the like. There isn't much else to the place, except a small storehouse and a smaller woodshed sitting next to the main building, and those give it a little more protection from storms, I suppose. Come to think of it, it isn't much bigger than this place."

"Where is it?' Catherine asked.

"Not too far off from here. It sits on top of the highest place in the area. A place called Table Hill," Richard said. "It won't be hard to find."

"Inspector, what hope do we have for rescue? The residents of Dawson must expect us to arrive at some point. Will they not send aid when we don't?"

Richard lowered his eyes to the floor. He couldn't bring himself to look at her when he said, "I never sent word of our visit to Dawson. I don't know who we can trust there, and I didn't want to forewarn Morgan of our arrival."

Catherine's swollen eyes shone with tears. She exhaled her words.

"Very well then. We'll have to try for the observatory. What other choice do we have?"

Chapter 10

The journey to the footbridge and then reconnecting with the trail had taken Azarov's party the rest of the day. Longer than any of them expected. Now, they stood inside a rest cabin. They used their torches to illuminate the inside, being careful to stand away from the entrance, so moonlight could shine through.

Knowing that the Mounties had gained equipment and provisions sent Azarov into a rage. It didn't help his mood when he noticed that several pages had been torn from the table's notebook and that the pencil was also missing. He had a guess as to what the Mounties had done and what they had in mind with those torn pages.

He cursed and overturned the table. The lamp smashed. The stink of oil filled the cabin, masking the smell of the blood that had soaked through the rags on the bunk. Azarov removed his hat and brushed his shaggy hair. Despite the cold, he was sweating.

"Boss, it looks like they had something to eat and moved on pretty quick. They must have a good lead on us now."

"I know that. That's why we can't afford to stay here for the night. We need to keep going."

None of his men grumbled when he said that, but Azarov could *feel* them grumbling. "This hunt can last another couple of hours or it can last another couple of days. It is up to us."

He pushed past the men and trudged out of the cabin. Kneeling next to the trail, he cursed the darkness and held his torch near the snow. He saw no blood in the Mounties' tracks.

"They may have done a good job of treating their wounds," he said, "but they are still hurt. Still tired and frightened."

The tracks were direct and purposeful. They gave no indication that the Mounties were deviating from the trail or doubling back. Good. Perhaps the Mounties did not even know they were still being followed.

Azarov searched the trail ahead. His eyes cast up and down tree trunks and bushes, looking for more clues. He saw broken branches and tufts of fur, but nothing that could help him. The lacework of snowshoes in fresh fallen snow told him that the Mounties certainly lay ahead of him, but their tracks had become mingled with those of his own men, left days before. Any other clues were hidden by these and the Yukon's long night.

Lottery knelt beside Azarov and said, "It won't be long now. The shape that they are in, we'll have no trouble chasing them down."

"Yes, we see that, so they must see it too. Why then do they run for Dawson?"

Azarov turned this over in his mind. He knew his prey was playing a ruse. There was no way the Mounties wanted to stay on the trail. They must have realized by now that there was no help or safety there.

So, how does their ruse work? he wondered.

Having just trekked this part of the trail, he knew nothing worth mentioning lay along the trail for another twenty miles.

Azarov stood and spread his arms. In a loud voice, he bellowed, "What's around here? I mean, off the trail."

"There is nothing 'round here, Captain," one man said. "Just trees."

Another spoke man spoke, "Well, there's an old mining camp about ten or fifteen miles from here. No one lives there now."

Azarov thought on this. "What else?"

"The observatory," Lang said.

Azarov turned to him but kept silent. Lang then described the observatory.

When he finished, he added, "Yeah, some Brit scientists built it about eight years ago. Well, they paid other men to build it for them."

"That's where they're going," Azarov said. "And that's where we're going."

Lang gritted his teeth and took a step towards Azarov, which Azarov took as more of an offence than a threat.

"What?!" Lang said. "But the book in the cabin said that — "

"Don't mind the damn book, Weasel," Lottery said. "The book is just a trick. The boss is smart. He knows a red herring when he sees one."

"Yes, I do," Azarov said. He knew when someone was kissing his ass too, but he let it go.

A thin smile crossed Azarov's face. "We have them now. Let's end this."

Before leaving, Azarov threw a lit match into the smashed lamp's oil. The cabin was engulfed in moments.

Lottery raised his eyebrows and looked at his boss. "Why'd you torch the place? It was a perfectly good cabin."

"That's why I torched it. I don't want any comforts that would entice us to turn back. Behind us, let there be nothing, Lottery. From now on, we move forward."

***

The clouds had vanished, and stars now freckled the indigo sky. The moon burned a hole through its middle. There was no need for their newly made torches. The light from above let Richard easily see the trail that their pursuers had already broken. The added brightness also exposed him and his companions. He looked up and wondered how long the clear sky would last.

He heard a branch snap, and he flattened himself against a birch tree. He signalled the others to stop. Holding his breath, he waited for the next sign, but none came. It must have been another branch breaking under the weight of the snow, he thought. He let himself breath again and pushed on.

His toes had been numb for an hour. Richard was certain he would have frostbite and considered stopping to examine his feet. Though, once he had his boots off, he was unsure how easy it would be to get them back on. He trudged forward, imagining his waxy, discoloured toes. If he reached the observatory quickly enough, perhaps they wouldn't need amputation. He moved faster.

Mike groaned. "That's it. I'm sorry, but I need to stop for a minute."

Richard and Catherine lowered him to the ground and leaned him next to a rock.

Mike scooped up a handful of snow and sucked it from his mitt. "Well, at least getting water isn't a problem for us."

"I'm not thirsty or warm enough to start gobbling up snow just yet," Catherine said.

Mike's breathing was heavy. It came in long, sucking draws, punctuated by a hiccupping sound.

"We can't keep going like this," he said. "The human body doesn't have the stamina for it. At least, not mine. I'm not going home, am I, Richard?"

Richard tried to sound sympathetic. Instead, he just croaked, "No, you're not going home. I'm sorry. I'm so sorry. God bless you."

"No surprise there. I swear, as soon as I took that bullet, I knew I would die out here sooner or later. Now, it is just happening later than I thought."

Richard was eager to break away from Mike. He stepped behind a tree to relieve himself, grateful to have something between the two of them.

"We know we can't beat them in a head-on fight" Mike called after him. "But perhaps we can thin their numbers enough to escape them. It would take a good deal of luck, which up to this point hasn't been on our side. But we may do it."

"What do you have in mind?" Catherine asked.

Mike lowered his voice and tried his best to look convincing. "Leave me behind. I'll walk off the trail, as deep into the woods as I can. They'll follow me. They'll have to because they can't afford to leave me behind in the rear."

A puzzled look crossed Catherine's face. "You want to split them off from the trail while we keep on it?" she said.

"Yes, I want you both to move up this trail as fast as you can. I can hold them off and delay them. Buy you some time. I think I can even get one or two of them for you."

"We can't leave you. We won't," she said.

Mike reached over and took her hand. "Catherine, you need to trust me. Our enemies expect us to run, not fight, so now is the time to fight."

All three of them were surprised at how quickly Richard unslung the rusted Winchester from his shoulder and handed over the rifle. He felt shame wash over his face, but he still managed to say, "I support your sacrifice, Constable. As commanding officer, I grant permission for you to stay."

Catherine glared at Richard.

Mike said nothing for a half-minute. He only stared into Richard's eyes. It was one of the longest moments of Richard's life. He knew how bad he looked. The guilt was crawling up his half-frozen feet, over his back and around to his reddened face.

"Coward," Catherine said. "You would leave Mike here so quickly?"

"I'm no coward, but I see the sense in his plan. At least some of them will follow his tracks and give us less of them to deal with. Hell, maybe they will all follow him."

"I can't believe I am hearing this from our group's leader," Catherine said. "We can't just leave him here."

"Catherine, it's my choice to stay. No one is abandoning me."

"Well, if you are so set on staying, then I will too. We're all probably going to die out here, but that doesn't mean that anyone needs to die alone. Inspector, do you have another gun?"

"I'm not a bloody armoury! Catherine, if we are to make the most of his sacrifice, we must leave now."

Richard tugged on her shoulder, and she opened her mouth to protest. Then Mike's eyes pleaded with her, and she kept silent. She turned away, choked out a sad sound, and stamped down the trail.

Mike looked up at Richard and forced a smile.

"God," he said. "What I wouldn't give right now to have my shotgun instead of this piece of shit."

He raised the Winchester and began checking it.

"And too bad that I never stayed behind back at the cabin. There, I could have stayed warm."

His teeth chattered, and his body shook. Richard knew that Mike did not have much time left. Soon, it wouldn't matter if he had stayed at the cabin, on the trail, or on a city street.

Richard gave him the flask he had taken from the cabin.

Mike chuckled, and said, "What's this? A rum ration to keep warm? Do you remember when they would give us rum rations to keep warm during cold nights in Africa?"

"Yes, I remember."

Mike opened the flask and took a belt. "I can feel my face getting hot. Thank you, Richard."

"Give them hell, Mike," Richard whispered.

He strode off after Catherine, not eager to hear from her again any time soon.

***

His party was gaining ground. He was sure of it. He had been pushing his men too hard for them not to be. He saw a disturbance in the fresh snow: tracks leading off the trail. Leaning close, Azarov could see the snowshoes' thong pattern. They were the tracks of only one person.

Azarov was sure of it. One of the Mounties had broken from the group.

The Mountie was easy to track. The moonlight exposed his massive prints. The trees held on to their cracked limbs, marking his passing. Most were bent in the direction in which he had fled, almost as if they were pointing, wanting their assailant to be caught.

Azarov never spoke. He hoped the dullest of his men understood what was happening. One Mountie had sacrificed himself. It was likely a wounded one. He had diverted the hunters away from the others. This game wouldn't last long. He imagined the Mountie as tired, staggering, afraid, and knowing that death was upon him.

How far could the hurt man travel? Azarov wondered. He felt a slight sadness. It would soon be time to perform the most unpleasant part of his livelihood.

"One of them must have lost his nerve," Lang said. "Now, he's trying to hide off the trail. Why don't we leave this one be? This has already turned out to be more trouble than we expected, and, if any of them make it to the observatory, we'll have to kill the people there too. Damn, we won't be able to cover up all that."

"Azarov, if the reverend talked," Lang continued, "then all of Fort MacCammon probably knows about the gold heist anyway. We can cut our losses and — "

And there it was. Azarov knew it would again come down the railway tracks for a second time. Oh, it never pulled into the station on time, but he knew the call for backing out had been coming. Azarov said nothing. Lang was smart enough to know this meant that his words hadn't swayed the Russian.

"All right, then," Lang said. "Fair enough. If you want this man dead so bad, then let's at least split up. Why don't I take some of the men and go in there after him? You take the rest after the other Mountie."

Azarov didn't like the sound of that plan. He could tell that the men were getting restless. This was already turning out to be more complicated than anyone expected. If he took his eyes off them, they might desert him. The idea of leaving them alone, with Lang of all people, to sow more seeds of betrayal in their minds was too much.

Azarov pointed to the newfound tracks. "No, let's not split. I don't want to give him a fighting chance. We all follow him together and finish him together. How dangerous can one hurt Mountie be?"

***

Mike thought about Africa. There, he worried about the heat and thirst. Now he wished for one breeze of that dry air on his face. How could one man find himself fighting for his life in two such extreme places during one lifetime? He dismissed the thought, as it was unbecoming of a real soldier or a real Mountie to bemoan such hardships.

He turned his ear towards the path he had made in the snow. He listened for the crunch of footsteps or the rustle of gear against clothing. He listened for whispers and soft breathing. He listened.

Nothing.

He had stopped walking only ten minutes from the trail. They should be upon him by now. He ground his teeth, a habit that annoyed him but was uncontrollable when he was tense. He did not have very long until his injuries finally finished him. He wished he could tell his enemies to hurry.

Mike questioned just how good a shot he would be. His marksmanship was satisfactory. It wasn't as good as when he was a military man, but he hunted often. Taking ducks on the wing and fleet-footed rabbits was what he called stress shooting, the sort of shooting one needs to master in order to shoot well under pressure. Regardless, there was the damned wound. How that would tamper with his aim, he had to wonder.

Mike lowered his head against the downed spruce that was hiding him. He was nestled between this fifteen-hundred-pound giant and a collection of boulders. The natural fortress made a good place to make a last stand.

And a final stand it would be. There was no more running. There was no aid just over the next hill. He was going to die here and now. It was only a matter of how much damage he could do to the enemy before they finished him. He thought again of Africa, of the day he saw a pack of hyenas taking down a lion. With the other soldiers, he watched in fascination and placed bets on how many hyenas the lion would cost their pack.

He closed his eyes to rest them for a moment only. Once they were rested, he would be more alert. He had almost drifted off to sleep when he heard the crunch of a single footstep. His enemies had arrived. Looking forward, he saw black shapes weaving in the darkness. The hyenas had come for him.

For the first time, he saw his hunters in detail. He counted seven of them, all armed. He watched for a sign that indicated which man was their leader, just as he had learned while in the army. But none wore any marks of distinction. Finally, one man stopped in his tracks, and when he did so, the six surrounding him did as well.

"That's you. Azarov. You're the leader of their damned little pack," Mike murmured to himself.

He put Azarov in his sights, but the alternative was too tempting. Two of the men had lined up single file. Mike shifted his rifle to them, and it roared. Its bullet slammed into the first man's upper chest and then through to the lower abdomen of the man behind him.

I hit them both, Mike thought. *Oh, my God in heaven, I actually hit them both.*

Two down with only one shot. If only he could make all his bullets count like that.

The shot sent Azarov behind a thick pine. His men did likewise. Muzzle flashes lit the night. It wasn't difficult for them to see where the shooter was hiding. Bullets scraped the bark of the spruce's trunk and sent splinters high in the air.

Mike burned through the rifle's magazine and never bothered to reload. There was no time. He grabbed his pistol and emptied it. In the detonating night, it was impossible to tell if he was hitting anyone. Mike opened his pistol's cylinder and fished out the spent cartridges. Smoke poured out as he rammed in fresh ammunition.

As the men's gunfire intensified, Mike saw something moving at the edge of his vision. He turned to face a shadow that took form as it closed over him. It was Azarov. The Russian had swept to Mike's left and made his way through the thick bush and boulder.

Azarov fired his pistol. Mike felt his body slump back against rocks. Two more shots tore into his chest and put Mike prostrate.

The fight was over. Somewhere in the distance, a wolf howled.

Chapter 11

"I told you that the Mountie would turn out to be too much trouble," Lang said.

A grumble came from the others, and it was much louder than Azarov cared for. He was losing control now. What bothered him just as much was that he knew Lang had been right. He needed to end this fast.

Azarov brought the butt of his revolver across Lang's jaw. It sent him into the snow on his ass. Azarov stood over the man and pointed the gun at the man's face.

"You cowardly turd. If I did not need you now, I would blow your nose out the back of your damned head," Azarov said. He spoke up so all of his men could hear him. "I don't want any more cowards' talk from anyone. We are going to hunt those Mounties down and finish this. The next man who talks about cutting our losses gets the other end of my gun."

Azarov let silence hang in the air to punctuate his point. Their expressions told him that they agreed, or at least understood.

He walked over to the wounded man, whose belly had been blown out by the Mountie's first shot. The man lay still on the ground. Even in the darkness, Azarov could see blood spreading across the snow. No one had bothered to treat him. *Perhaps they knew that it didn't matter for this one*, Azarov thought.

He leaned down and retrieved the man's rifle. A few brushes removed the snow. After checking its magazine, he left one round in, chambered.

"Please. Don't leave me like this," the wounded man said. He wasn't so much speaking the words as he was exhaling them. "Will you bury me, at least?"

"We can't. We need to get back on the trail if we are to catch the rest of them. We've already lost enough here."

Lottery could not hide his disgust. "What? We can't just leave him to die out here. He'll bleed out and freeze. No man deserves a slow death."

The look Azarov shot him was enough to shut his mouth.

In a soft voice, he said to the wounded man, "Sorry, but we have to go. Whenever you're ready, you be a man and do what's right."

He then handed the wounded man the rifle and turned his back on him. Not for a second did he fear that the man would put the bullet in his back.

Azarov stood and reassumed his stern tone.

"The rest of you, come!"

He turned and made his way back to the main trail. Without a word, they followed. Only Lottery whispered a farewell to the man. Azarov and his four remaining men had travelled a thousand feet before they heard a gunshot behind them.

***

"They followed Mike. I'm sure of it," Richard called over his shoulder.

"How can you tell? Catherine said.

"Otherwise, they would be on top of us by now. I'm certain that Mike took at least a couple of them down with him. He had them beat in fighting skills and experience, guaranteed. From what I saw, Azarov's party is just brainless louts living by the gun. But if you are going to choose an occupation like that, you had better know how to handle a weapon. I'm sure Mike taught them a thing or two.

"Why haven't we heard any gunfire?" Catherine said.

"This whole time, I expected to hear some over those foothills behind us, but nothing. We must have travelled so far that we didn't hear it."

He and Catherine had turned off the trail an hour earlier and were now on the path to the observatory. The snow was higher here, pushing the pair upwards close to the tops of the lower trees. Both of them could benefit from a break, but they kept climbing. Hill streams ran down the white-crowned slopes, carving their way through the snow. Occasionally, Richard and Catherine would have to hop over a narrow stream, or if it was too wide, search for a slim place to cross.

He remembered his last trip to the observatory and tried to recall landmarks. In the dark, he was unsuccessful. The only signage on the path was the wooden sign that had hung at the turnoff to the observatory. As he passed the sign, he tore it down and tossed it far away from the trail.

If only they had a heavy snowfall now, it would cover their tracks. Richard sighed and counted what blessings they had. The sky had started to cloud over after all, and he hoped the darkness would conceal them.

"It's so dark now. If they aren't great trackers, then maybe they'll miss our tracks at the junction." He hoped he sounded optimistic.

"I doubt that. There is no way they can lose our tracks," Catherine said. "With these big snowshoe prints, a child could follow us. Maybe we can split up and rejoin later. It will be harder for them to follow two trails at once. Is that not so?"

"Too dangerous," Richard replied. "Splitting up means that one of us needs to leave this trail. That means one of us is bound to get lost out there."

His thoughts were interrupted by the sound of rushing water. Ahead, he saw a creek foaming against the high banks that flanked it. He was eager to clear the creek quickly and let the trees and shadows on the opposite bank embrace him. He and Catherine sat on the creek's bank and loosened their boots from their snowshoes.

"Don't lose those in the creek. Without your snowshoes you'll sink hip-deep into a snowdrift and be trapped," Richard said.

While taking his own snowshoes off, Richard stared at the creek. He wondered how much gold lay in its bed. If he had made different choices in his life, how much could he have taken out of there? He imagined his pockets bulging with gold dust.

Richard carefully negotiated his way across the creek's slick rocks. He took his time crossing. One false step would put him in the water. In this cold, and with no shelter in sight, that would mean death.

Once across, Richard decided it was a good time to break and observe. He had made it a habit to periodically stop and listen for Azarov's party. Sometimes, he thought he heard a muffled voice or the crunch of feet in snow. He hoped it was the wind playing tricks on him.

From this height, he could see through the trees and over the hillside. He surveyed a mile-wide gulley that they had passed through only an hour before. The moonlight against the sheen of the ice gave him enough illumination to search for the chasers. He removed his field glasses from their case and peered through them, adjusting their focus. Any moment, he expected their pursuers to emerge from the spruce trees that lay beyond the gulley, but no one came. Satisfied that Azarov's party was not close behind him, Richard slid his field glasses back into his case.

He tried to read the minds of the men hunting him. They were surely cocky. They had already wiped out most of his party and must believe that the remainder had little chance. He looked about the gloomy woods, now more haunting in the vanishing moonlight.

It isn't a nice looking place to die, but where is? he thought.

The wind was picking up now. Whenever Richard blinked, his eyelids felt wet from the snow brushing them. It reminded him of the risk of exposure. Without proper shelter, or at least a fire, he knew they only had a few hours left to live.

And the steep hill wasn't doing any favours to his worn legs. Richard imagined himself finally collapsing into a snowbank, his legs as loose as ropes. His gums puffy and red from malnourishment. His belly churning with hunger pangs. Who was he fooling? The hunters would kill him and Catherine long before then. Fatigue was finally taking its toll. Eventually, legs and lungs would fail them, and then he and Catherine would be taken.

"No matter. I can't think about the bad things. I need to concentrate on the good." Richard's hamstrings trembled and each step was uncertain. "At least I have my snowshoes."

Richard thought about his deceased wife. Rose would tell him an optimistic attitude was most important. Richard had never taken this advice seriously before, but he knew he needed to now. If he was going to endure the coming hardships, he needed to stay positive.

"If you get out of bed every morning thinking that the day will be lousy, it will be."

"What's was that?" Catherine asked. Richard hadn't realized that he had been thinking aloud.

"Nothing, Catherine. Just keep your eyes on me, and I will keep my eyes on the trail."

He turned to see how well she was keeping pace with him. She had slowed down and was trying to walk while brushing away their tracks with a tree branch. She swung it from side to side, like she was sweeping with a broom. It was pointless. The effort only made their trail more visible. Also, it was slowing them down. Richard was certain of two things. First, their chasers would be upon them soon if he and Catherine kept moving at this rate. Second, he couldn't leave her behind. Not after Mike. Not after the others.

"Aren't you worried about going to the observatory, Inspector? Will that not put its residents in danger?"

"Yes, it will," he said. "After a short siege, our pursuers will likely burn us out. As for the unfortunate scientists living there, they could be killed. I can't stomach the idea of endangering them. Those are good men. I know them. Duran and Bouchard are their names. It's routine for the Winter Patrol to stop at the observatory and check on their safety. Usually, we accept their hospitality and stay the night. It breaks my heart to be leading Azarov to Duran and Bouchard. As heavy as this load is, it is our burden. We would shoulder it alone."

To his right, fifty paces, he saw an opening in a ridge. In the darkness, he would have missed the cave, if not for a bird flying out of it. Richard could immediately tell that it would provide shelter. As relief filled him, he wondered whether it was luck, or perhaps it truly was a blessing from God.

"Thank God," he said.

The cave opening was only a few feet wide, but it looked almost high enough for Richard to walk through fully upright. A wall of icicles sheeted the entrance. Richard smashed his way to the interior. The cave's depth was a surprising sixty feet, which gave adequate protection against the biting wind. The granite walls and floor were dry, which was another mercy.

Richard waved his torch downwards. "It looks like we aren't the first to use this place as a shelter," he said.

The light revealed lumps of fur and bones littering the cave's bottom. They also saw the remains of a long-extinguished campfire. A few sticks of dry wood lay beside the charred ones. This was a morsel of luck, since neither of them had gathered wood while travelling.

"Let's count our blessings," Catherine said. "I didn't think we would be stopping to rest at all, let alone stopping in a place that had a little firewood."

"I didn't know that this place was here. By God, I would have had my men put a cache of supplies in here years ago."

He immediately got to the business of lighting a fire. With a torch already lit, the rest was easy. Soon, the cave filled with the fire's warmth and smoke.

"Well, at least the fire will keep away the four-legged predators," he muttered.

He removed the last of their food from his sack: a can of beans. He placed it next to the fire. When they left Mike, he thought of reaching over to take from Mike's sack. A dying man wouldn't need it. However, Richard couldn't bring himself to do it. For him, it would have been like premature grave robbing.

But he knew that Catherine and he wouldn't last long without food. They were exhausting themselves too quickly, and the human body needs a superabundance of fuel to burn to keep warm in frigid temperatures. Without adequate food, their bodies would quickly slacken and then break like unwound clocks.

While waiting for the beans to warm, Richard reached into his pack and removed the pages and pen that he had taken from the cabin. He leaned close to the pages so he could see them in the dimness. He stirred the fire with a stick to brighten the cave.

"Do you really think writing all this down will make a difference?"

"We need to place our faith in something."

"What about God?"

Richard never missed a penstroke. "Pray to him if you want. He and I haven't conversed in a long time. I would sooner place my faith in a glass of scotch. I wish I had a drink now."

Richard caught the way she stared at him. Even in their situation, she still had time for disapproval.

"Only to calm my nerves," he added.

"Only as a way to escape is what you mean," she said.

She was right, and he knew it. That's all the drinking had ever been for him. A way out of reality.

"What the hell are we going to do," Catherine finally said. "Even if we reach the observatory, we will only be cornering ourselves and endangering the men there." She sobbed. "What in God's name are we going to do? I wish we could just stay in here." She paused. "I need a gun."

"The hell you do. You're liable to shoot one of us with it."

"I know how to handle a pistol. Walter taught me when we first moved north. Richard, you are going to need all the help you can get."

Richard sighed and reached into his pack. He pulled out the spare pistol, the Enfield, and was grateful to be lightening his load. "I can see you aren't going to let this go, and I'm too tired to fight."

He gave it to her. Its bulk made the gun look humorous in her delicate hands. But she pointed it in a safe direction and checked its cylinder. Satisfied that it was fully loaded, she closed the cylinder and stuffed the gun under her coat.

She does know how to handle a gun, he thought. He gave her a slight smile and said, "Who knows? Maybe you will use it to avenge Walter." Richard dropped the smile and bit his tongue. "I'm sorry, I…"

"No, it is all right. We've seen one unexpected thing after another on this journey, so maybe you are right. Maybe I can gain some sort of justice for him. Not retribution, but justice. I've always detested violence for the sake of reprisal, and, as a nurse, I have always worked to heal people. But there must be justice for my husband, and now that I have the means to it in my hands, seeing it delivered feels like more of a necessity than a want. I suppose that sounds mad to you, Richard."

"Not at all. I believe that there are three types of justice in this world. There is the justice granted by the courts. There is the justice given by God. And then there is the shit that you need to take for yourself."

He leaned over and touched the gun in her hand, stroking the barrel. "Let's see if together, we can strike the blow for Walter."

A draft blew through the cave's opening, and Richard trembled. "I swear, if I survive this, I'll move someplace hot. Maybe I'll go to the American southern states. Florida, perhaps."

"Florida? I've heard that's all swampland," Catherine said.

"So, what of it? Dawson City was built on a swamp, and people call it one of the nicest places to live in Canada.

Besides, I would rather take my chances with the alligators than put up with this shit."

Richard pulled off his bandage and examined his arm. The bullet had left a long cut, but it looked worse than it was. It wasn't deep, and his arm still had full movement. He searched his belongings for anything that would suffice as a clean bandage. Still, he knew how difficult it was to keep a wound clean while in the wilderness.

"You better let me look at that," Catherine said.

"I can take care of it myself."

"Please, I want to be useful."

"All right, but make sure you bandage it well. If I leave a blood trail, they'll think I'm too hurt to put up a real fight. They'll rush in for the killing blow."

She moved across the fire to sit against the cave's wall. She expertly took his arm and studied the wound while preparing a dressing. Richard poked at the can of beans by the fire, paying no attention to her.

"How strange it is that you of all people should end up here," she said.

"What do you mean, 'you of all people'?"

"I mean, here in the north. In this cave. It's no secret. Everyone in Fort MacCammon knows how unhappy you are."

"They do? And what else do they know? Do they know what a drunk I am?"

"I won't lie to you. People have noticed things." Catherine paused, as if not knowing how to follow that. "I've never had problems with heavy drinking myself, but I've heard that it's like falling into a hole."

"Drunkenness isn't a hole. It's a slope with a very gentle grade. Every drink you take is another step downwards. Then one day, you look behind and see how damn low you have put yourself and wonder if you will ever get back to where you were.

"Now, take a good, honest look at me, lady. At forty-one, a man doesn't just bounce back from a serious bout of drunkenness — not in the Mounties. What with the standards for performance being what they are. And the demands placed on you by the service. It's a challenge for a good Mountie, and what sort of Mountie am I now? I walked my patrol into a trap and then fled. I left a man behind to make a brave, last stand. A real Mountie would have stood beside him. You were right when you called me a coward, Catherine. I wonder what Rose would think if she saw me today. Maybe she would just see a pitiful drunk still failing the people around him. I wasn't there for her when she died either."

Catherine sighed. "Richard, my words were unkind and untrue. I'm sorry. And even if they were true, then they wouldn't matter at this moment. The Royal North West Mounted Police needs you now. Dawson City needs you. I need you. My God, don't you think that is what your wife would have wanted? For you to stand up and serve? And what about what you want, Richard? Don't you want a grain of respect and whatever it was you had when she was still alive?"

"When she was alive, what I had was her, and I can never get that back. So, let's talk about something else."

Catherine's eyes told Richard that she regretted mentioning Rose.

"I'm sorry, Inspector," she said. "I've no right to use your deceased wife as a weapon to convince you."

"It's all right. You never meant anything by it. Forget it."

Exasperation boiled in Richard's throat. He brushed the can of beans out of the fire, and, after a few moments, pried away its lid. He offered some to Catherine, and, to his surprise, she refused. He let the can cool and then pawed its contents into his mouth. He wondered if this would be his last meal.

For the first time in a long time, Richard wanted to pray to God. It was not that he had ever rejected the Lord, but, after his wife's death, he wondered if God had rejected him. If so, what could have made him lose God's love? He quickly struck these thoughts from his mind. It was fear and desperation overtaking him, nothing more. He lay his head against his pack and shut his eyes.

"Richard, I have something to tell you," Catherine said. From the sound of her voice, Richard knew that it couldn't be good.

"I'm carrying a baby." She touched her belly, and the gesture made a belt tighten around Richard's neck. Once his throat relaxed, he still couldn't talk. The truth was that he didn't know what to say. She clearly wasn't joking. Saying that it was a tragedy, given circumstances, would be stating the obvious. And he didn't have any solutions.

He looked down at her fur coat and wondered how pregnant she was under there. "How far along are you?"

"Five months."

"Five months! How the hell did you keep it hidden for so long?"

"Well, tall women carry babies without showing very much ... and ... well, I'm tall."

He looked at her again, and considered all the layers of clothes that women wear in the north. Yes, he could believe that she was pregnant. No wonder Walter was so protective, but now that onus for protection fell on Richard's shoulders. Richard had led Walter to his grave, and so Richard was now saddled with the burden of safeguarding his family.

"Why did you come on the journey? You must have known that the trail is no place for a woman bearing a child."

"I did, but Walter told me I would be more unsafe if I stayed at the fort. I had no choice, he said. He told me to think of our unborn baby."

Despite her protests, Richard eventually got her to eat the can of beans by appealing to her maternal sentiments. "You need to eat to keep up your strength, for the sake of the baby," he said.

After the last bite, the two sat for the next five minutes. Catherine stared at the fire, the only source of comfort that either of them had. "Well, that's it then," Richard said.

"There's the tipping point right there. Between everything that I owe to people, your safety, and now the baby, there is just too much at stake. I need to get you and that baby to safety. And then, I swear that I'll put an end to Morgan."

Richard pulled her closer to him and whispered in her ear. "We can't stay here. Even if they miraculously miss us, we'll freeze to death or die of pneumonia. We need to keep going, pushing towards the observatory. Get some rest, Catherine. We'll leave in a couple of hours."

Chapter 12

Two hundred feet ahead, the trail bent to the left. Beyond the bend, Azarov could hear rushing water. He was sure that his quarry had made its way across some waterway that lay ahead. Azarov could soon see a brook. Its fast-flowing waters looked cold and refreshing. Azarov hadn't realized how thirsty he was until now. The roar of the water became louder, and he wondered if he would hear his prey over the sound.

He reached the water's edge with his two men close behind. Large, rounded stones stuck out of the creek. He didn't bother to state to his men that the Mounties used these to cross, dry-footed, to the opposite bank. Near the water's edge, the men could see body prints where the Mountie kneeled to drink and to remove his snowshoes. There were similar prints on the opposite bank.

Azarov plunged his canteen into the swift water and sloshed it down his parched throat. He wiped his mouth with his sleeve and stared ahead. He wondered if his prey had laid a trap for them. If he could ambush Mounties, could Mounties ambush him? He dismissed this as a long shot. The Mounties may have uncommon tenacity, but they were wounded and frightened. No, they were still running.

Soon after, the tracks led Azarov's party to the cave. His prey would have been lucky if they hadn't found a bear already inside. Azarov gestured to Lang to enter first.

"Why don't you lead?" Lang said.

"Have you ever seen a man after he stumbled onto a bear's home?"

"No."

"I have."

Lang grudgingly lowered himself and cautiously crept into the cave. The more likely threat was that the Mounties could still be in there. Yet, all they found were the remains of a campfire. Azarov circled the ashes, studying them. He saw the burnt-out bean can beside it. He was sure that it would be the Mounties' last supper. Azarov stirred the ashes with his boot and placed his hand near them. He could still feel the embers' heat.

"How far ahead do you think they are?" Lottery asked.

"Not too far. Their fire is still hot. Two hours, perhaps. But I don't think we will catch them before sunrise," Azarov replied.

Azarov thought about the people he was following, noticing that, gradually, he was seeing them more as people rather than prey. What sort were they? He guessed that they must have nice families at home in order to keep themselves going up to this point. Or perhaps it was their faith that was letting them endure. Even if God was unreal, faith in the Lord was a powerful motivator. In any case, Azarov felt some admiration for the Mounties.

"These Mounties have … what do you call it?" When people should stop but do not stop?"

"Heart," Lottery replied.

That wasn't the fancy word that Azarov had in mind, but it was suitable.

"Yes," he said. "They have heart."

***

They welcomed the sunrise. The change in temperature, ever so slight, was noticeable to each man. Fortune was once again with Azarov's party. They had lost the path in the darkness, but now regained it. The lacework of the Mounties' snowshoes was clear with the morning light. Azarov had already ordered his men not to speak, but once every hundred yards, he held up his hand, signalling them to stop moving and listen.

They moved over the cresting snowdrifts and between patches of pine trees, sloping upwards towards the hilltop. Soon, they would reach the observatory. He imagined the observatory as Lang had described it. Small and plain with a thin trail of smoke rising from its chimney. Azarov could swear that, even now, he could smell roasting rabbit through his frozen nose hairs. After the Mounties and the unfortunate men in the observatory were dead, he would warm himself by the fire and have his fill.

Azarov wondered what the Mounties had in store, and he wondered what he would do if he were in their place. He smiled and thought, *No matter. Little tricks will not save them now*.

The Mounties' tracks were closer together than they were before.

They are weakening, Azarov thought. They are almost dragging themselves along at this point.

He could now see a ridge one hundred feet ahead, and somewhere beyond that lay his enfeebled game.

"Look at the tracks, Lottery. The tracks are changing," Azarov said. "They are not as neat as they used to be. Do you see how messy and ruined the edges are? The tracks are getting closer together too."

The prints were no longer well-defined. Their edges had crumbled, as if the Mounties were dragging their snowshoes, now shuffling through the snow.

"They're getting tired," Lottery said.

Azarov only smiled and nodded. He was about to finish them off, with no exceptions. Morgan would never tolerate them surviving at this point. It was best to get it over with and head back to Dawson. And if anything was certain about this day, it was that these murders would be the last tasks that Azarov fulfilled for Morgan. No matter the threats against his wife and children, Azarov was going to pack up the family as soon as he could hurry back to them. Morgan's reign wouldn't survive all of this. Azarov was sure of that. He had to move his family quickly, or they would be caught in the collapse of Morgan's empire.

Azarov drew a breath to give his next order when all of them heard a crunch in the snow behind them. They turned in unison to see a Mountie standing eighty feet behind them, on top of a colossal snowdrift. In his right hand, he held a pistol pointed down towards them. In his other hand, he held a hatchet.

There was something that did not look right with the Mountie. It was his snowshoes. They were green, and they stuck out in front of him. It all became so clear to Azarov.

Shit! Azarov thought. *He strapped pine boughs to his feet as snowshoes. He used them to circle around behind us! He had been behind us all the time.*

Azarov saw that the Mountie wasn't panicking. With the high-ground advantage and his gun already brought to bear on them, the Mountie had reason to be confident. What Azarov saw was a man who knew that the time for running was over. He saw a man who was unafraid.

***

Richard couldn't bring himself to endanger the men at the observatory. So, he took a risk and his stunt had worked. His makeshift pine snowshoes had eased his way over the snowdrifts. Without them, one step on the high snowdrifts would put him deep in the snow, stuck and vulnerable.

To his left, Catherine hid behind a tree. Like him, she had traded her snowshoes for pine boughs. She pressed herself against the trunk and peeked at the stirring battle.

"Stay there!" Richard called to her. "Just stay where you are!"

The last thing he wanted was her getting in the way and ruining whatever little chance they had for survival.

Below, he saw Azarov. Even though he had met the Russian only once, years ago, he recognized him now. The man's squat body and Asiatic features were still clear to

Richard. Apart from the Russian, Richard counted four other men.

The men had fallen for his false trail. It was too neat — too easy — for them to pass up. It bred the overconfidence that Richard had hoped for. Their arrogance and stupidity had ripened with each step, and now with high ground, a clear line of fire, and his gun trained on the men floundering about below, he had the advantage. It was Richard's time to harvest what he had grown. The Mountie pulled the trigger and unleashed his storm.

The first shot should have been an easy one. Richard's Colt sang, and a man's face disappeared in a red mist. It wasn't the face he was aiming for, however. He wanted to kill Azarov first, but as he fired on the Russian, one of his companions stepped in the way.

Oh well, a downed man is a downed man, Richard conceded. And that man was certainly down. His body convulsed in the snow, as if the gunfight needed to get any more bizarre.

He glanced towards Catherine, still trying her best to hide behind the tree. It cost him. Richard was too slow to bring his gun to bear on Azarov. The Russian had taken cover behind the nearest pine. The man whom Richard had heard Azarov call Lottery would have to do. The next round from Richard's pistol slammed into the right side of the wounded man's face and the left side exploded outwards. He dropped into a nearby snowdrift.

That was when one man lost his control and began panic-firing. He shot from the hip, and waved his rifle at the trees, as if he were trying to erase them. His hand worked the rifle's lever-action so quickly that nothing could be heard over the rifle's roar. Hot shell casings spat out into the cold air. No soldier worth his army boots would waste his ammunition in such reckless fashion. *A couple of years in the army could have saved him today*, Richard thought.

The gunfire was an unsteady drumming. Richard saw a rabbit dart from its hiding place. A crow flew from its cover and crossed in front of him. *This whole damn forest is losing its mind*, he thought.

One bullet missed Richard's left shoulder by at least eight feet and a tree branch split behind him, but Richard stood his ground. He wouldn't be lunging for cover this time. Pivoting to his left, Richard emptied his revolver. The man screamed and danced in the snow. His cries and jigging ceased, and he fell.

Three men down, and he hadn't been killed. Richard soared. He opened the cylinder of his revolver and removed the hot casings. Before he could ram in fresh cartridges, the last of Azarov's men charged him. His own ammunition spent, the man drew his knife from its sheath and howled as he ran for Richard. The seven-inch blade on the knife was chipped and blackened by tree sap, charred wood, and all the other dirty things in the woods. It would surely give a filthier cut than Richard's axe.

And Richard recognized the knife's holder. Constable Arnold Lang. Richard had always disliked Lang — he thought the man a bastard — but it was still a surprise to see any Mountie standing with Azarov. Even in that scorching instant, a small measure of disappointment at seeing a Mountie among his enemies crept into Richard.

But if there was one thing that living in the north had taught Richard, it was how to swing an axe. He swung his hatchet just as Lang came upon him. Richard's timing was perfect. The axe head and half of the axe handle landed against Lang's torso. Richard heard something inside of the man crack.

Ribs. Oh God, those are ribs, Richard thought. Yes, the ribs were broken, their splinters probably embedded into the vital organs behind them.

Lang wheezed and his eyes rolled into the back of his head. He gurgled something out of his mouth that sounded like he may have been trying to say Richard's name, but Richard had no care for that. Lang convulsed and spat hot blood across Richard's face. In disgust, Richard grabbed the back of Lang's head by the hair and crashed him into the snow. Lang didn't move, and Richard was confident that he never would again.

Richard had just enough time to turn his thoughts towards Azarov, when a bullet shattered the bark of the tree next to him. The near miss raked splinters across his cheek, even though the cold had numbed his face. He saw Azarov emerge from behind a pine. The Russian had him clear in his sights. Yet, Azarov did not fire. Richard realized that the near miss was not a miss at all, but a warning shot. Richard froze, waited, and watched.

Azarov held his fire and took a step closer.

"Drop the gun," Azarov said. "It is no good to you. We both know it is empty, or why would you use the axe?"

Richard complied.

"I know you. From the whaling station, a couple of years ago. Inspector Richard Carol, yes?"

"Yes, and you're Vadim Azarov," Richard said.

Hearing his name made Azarov smile. As if reading Richard's mind, Azarov said, "I'm not going to kill you just yet because I need you."

"What for?"

"For answers. What happened to the reverend? Did he die?"

"Yes. Were you the one who shot him?"

"It won't matter to you if I did or did not. What did he tell you?"

"Nothing. He died before anyone could question him."

"Is that why you left for Dawson so quickly? Because he told you nothing? You damn liar. He told you everything. He told you about Morgan and his business."

"Business? That's a poor choice of words for the enterprise that he built," Catherine said, stepping away from her tree.

You damn fool, Richard thought. Until then, she had gone unnoticed by Azarov.

Azarov turned to face her. "Come here," he said. "Now. I will not say again."

She did not move until he aimed his revolver towards her, and then she walked over to Richard. She reached over and took his hand. Richard knew that it was something that a person does when they believe they are about to die. "You see, Inspector? I knew that the reverend told you," Azarov said. "And who did you tell? I'm guessing all of Fort MacCammon knows about Morgan and his dealings by now."

"I told no one. I didn't know who I could trust at the fort."

"No more lies from you. You've probably already sent word south."

"If you believe that, then killing us won't help Morgan now. But killing us would hurt you."

"Not hardly. All of my men are dead. Most of your people are dead too. If I finish you two, then who is left to implicate old Vadim?"

The Russian smiled again, but this time, it was the smile of a chess player who was about to announce "checkmate."

"Besides, by the time your bodies are found and Mounties are sent to Dawson, my family and I will have left the Yukon. We will finally be away from Morgan and all the damn problems that come with him. There is one last problem that we must settle. I want your writings."

"Writings?"

Azarov cocked his pistol. "Please, we will not play this game, Inspector. Throw them on the ground, and we will finish this unfortunate affair with as much dignity as we can."

Richard removed the notes from his food sack and tossed them in the snow. His mind raced. He needed another card to play, but couldn't find one.

This time, I've come up short, he thought.

Azarov exhaled with relief. He leaned down to retrieve the papers from the ground.

From the corner of his eye, Richard caught a flicker of movement. He turned to his left just in time to see Catherine seizing her chance. She snuck her hand into the folds of her coat and pulled out the gun that Richard had given her.

Azarov had time only to raise his head and see his fate coming.

She aimed and fired so fast that Richard was certain that she missed. But the bullet slammed into Azarov's chest, just below the diaphragm. He made a woofing sound and crumpled over into the snow. He didn't move.

"Catherine, are you all right?" Richard said. Catherine only stood there, still pointing the Enfield at Azarov.

Richard stepped to her. He was careful not to get into her line of fire.

"It's all right. It's all over now," he said as he took the gun from her. "They can't hurt us anymore. You see? All of our chasers lay dead around us." On cue, Richard heard a gurgling coming from Azarov. The man's face shone with blood in the morning sunlight. Richard stepped towards him and thought about the Boer boy he shot in Africa so long ago. There would be no medical aid today. No chivalrous actions worthy of war medals. All that was left to give were bullets and the finality that came with them.

Richard lowered his pistol and cocked the hammer. Azarov stared at Richard and said, "I don't deserve this."

"None of us do," Richard replied and sent a bullet spinning through Azarov's forehead.

Richard told himself that he had ended a man's suffering, and what little mercy there was to be given that day was given in that.

He turned to face Catherine and her condemnation. Instead, her expression was one of acceptance.

"You did the right thing," she said.

Richard took the true meaning of her words. She was telling him that she would have done the same thing if she were him.

Azarov and his men were now even less of a threat than the silent wilderness that sprawled around all of them. Richard took Catherine in his arms. She let out one of her choking sobs that Richard was now accustomed to hearing. The tears began. She drew a breath and let out a wail, and

Richard was sure that the men in the nearby observatory heard it, just as surely as they had heard that gun battle. Soon, her crying was the only sound in the whole forest.

***

After regaining a scrap of composure, Richard and Catherine made their way to the observatory, cold, hungry, exhausted, and desperate for aid. Richard was worried about Catherine and her baby and gave no thought to himself. As difficult as it was for him to endure these hardships, he knew that it must be close to unbearable for a woman carrying a child.

It wasn't long before Richard and Catherine were in sight of the observatory. Its two inhabitants stared out of the building's window. They hid themselves behind its curtain. Though he couldn't see the guns, Richard knew the men were holding them.

Once the pair recognized Richard, they lowered their guard and raced to open the door. Richard never made it, though. Thirty feet from the observatory, he fell into the snow.

Richard felt the power flush from his body. For the first time in a long time, he allowed his muscles and mind to relax. As the relief washed through him, the strength washed out. He lay face down in the snow, undisturbed there in a sea of cool blackness. Richard was taken by a feeling of peace in those few moments before he lost consciousness.

Chapter 13

It took a long time for him to awaken. Richard drifted in a half-sleep state for an hour. Even before he opened his eyes, he knew he was safe in the observatory. He could feel the mattress under him and a handmade blanket over him. When he finally roused himself, he saw that he was in the observatory's Spartan bedroom. It had two bunks and no decorations. The fur blankets on the mattresses were the closest things to luxuries.

Through the doorway, he saw the observatory's main living area. Clothes lay in piles. Dishes were unwashed. Duran and Bouchard were both unmarried, and neither had children. Richard supposed that their family situations suited their housekeeping habits and occupations. He could see a recent photograph of Queen Victoria hanging on a wall.

A man stepped into the doorway.

"You're awake," he said. "Finally. You have been asleep for a whole day."

Richard recognized Duran. The portly fellow beamed with happiness.

"Where's Catherine?" Richard said. "Is she all right?"

"Catherine is finishing up a meal in the kitchen. She was very tired when you arrived, as you were, but she seems to be recovering from your ordeal better. That's surprising, given her delicate condition."

"You know she's pregnant."

"How could you not tell? Once she removed her coat, it was obvious.

Duran stepped into the room and slowly lowered himself onto the opposite bunk. He moved with a caution that implied that Duran was still trying to decide how to approach Richard and the new crisis that had been thrown upon him. It wasn't so long ago that Richard felt that same way, when the reverend had first arrived at Fort MacCammon.

"She's fine. She told us all about what happened. The shot reverend, the death of her husband and the others, and everything else. This Morgan sounds like quite a challenge for you. For anyone. It's a shame that he did not disappear with the Gold Rush that built him.

Richard drew a breath knowing that his next moves would hurt. He eased himself up into a sitting position, and Duran waited until Richard was comfortable before continuing with what Richard was guessing would be a lengthy conversation.

"In a way, it's fitting that the greatest scoundrel born out of the Gold Rush would be so powerful to have survived the rush's demise. But there is one thing that I don't understand, Inspector. If you were chased by these men, why not reach the observatory and have Bouchard and I help you fight them?"

"It was my fight," Richard said.

He thought of how Catherine had been the one to shoot Azarov and save them both from execution. He added, "Mine and Catherine's, rather."

Richard touched his wounded arm. The fresh, clean bandages somehow looked out of place. He saw that the dirt of the trail had been cleaned away from his hands and arms. While he had been unconscious, they not only redressed his wound, but also washed him. He swore that he could still feel the sensation of hot water. They had cut his hair and shaved him as well. He could tell without even touching his head. He saw a small mirror by a basin in the adjacent room, but he knew he couldn't coax his sore muscles to it.

"Can I get that mirror?" he asked and pointed.

"Certainly," Duran said and left the room. He returned and gave the hand mirror to Richard. Richard saw his reflection — what his misadventure had done to him. It had only been four days since he had left the fort, but he could swear that he looked older. He touched his face. The bones were more pronounced along his jaw and cheeks, and his lips were cracked with red fissures. The only part of his face that didn't look worse were the eyes. Those eyes now sparkled in the bunkroom's scant light. A day of sleep had done them good. And, in them, Richard could see a steadiness. His commitment to his mission was unwavering.

"I certainly look worn, but that's of little concern," Richard said.

"Yes, I'm sure that after a few days of rest, you will be fine."

"I don't have a few days to spare. I need to get back on the trail and go to Dawson. I have a gold heist to stop."

"Yes, Catherine told us all about that too. So, what's your plan, Inspector?"

"I'm going to Dawson, and I'll apprehend Morgan before the heist happens."

"It's as simple as that?"

"Has anything been simple so far?"

"But Inspector, why not wait to catch the crooked devils in the act? You can go to Dawson and watch the bank. When the Mounties move the gold, you can follow. When the bandits try to steal the gold, you can step in and arrest both the guards and the bandits."

"Too dangerous," Richard said. "I don't know how many men and guns there will be. With only me against them, it would be hopeless. We would be lucky if they didn't execute me on the spot, steal the gold anyway, and then say that I was one of the bandits."

Duran's mouth opened slightly. His eyes widened. "Wait, what do you mean, 'only me'? I thought you would be heading back to Fort MacCammon for more men first. With all due respect — "

"Stop," Richard said. "I know what you're going to say. I'm in no shape to do this by myself. But I'm going anyway, and I'm going alone."

Duran frowned. He looked Richard up and down, like Richard was a pair of old shoes that he was considering for the trash.

"Forget the fight," he said. "You may not make it to Dawson at all! Inspector, your sense of duty is admirable, but it isn't worth your life. You can't just seize this Morgan fellow by yourself and put him in a cage. If this man is as powerful as Catherine explained, won't he have more of his men present to protect him? Surely, you must return to Fort MacCammon and get more Mounties."

"It would take too many days to travel back there and get help." Richard's head hurt and he wasn't in a mood to fight with Duran. Exasperated, he said, "Morgan is a smart man. He undoubtedly has a secondary plan in place, in case his plan to stop the reverend fails. I guarantee you, Duran, Morgan has a plan to blackmail someone else into taking the fall for him, or something equally sly. The only way to block his alternative plan is to charge towards him now. We need to reach him before he finds out that Azarov and his men have failed."

Duran nodded, and Richard took this as a sign that the man saw the sense in his argument.

Richard said, "I'm sure that he will have some more men, but I'll have to take my chances with them. It's a risky move, no doubt. But I figured that's all life has been for the last couple of days: one big gamble. Besides, I need to see this through by myself. Men died back there on the trail, and it was my fault. Do you understand?"

He glared at Duran harder than he wanted. Duran had helped him, and the man certainly didn't deserve Richard's attitude.

In a softer tone, he continued, "I left men to die. This isn't just about duty to the service. This is also about what I owe to *them*. If I need help, then I'll get help in Dawson," Richard said.

"From who? You said some of the other Mounties are already being paid off. How will you know who to trust? Is there anyone waiting for you in Dawson, Inspector? Someone who you can count on?" Duran straightened up and drew a breath. Richard knew what Duran was going to say next. "I'll have to come with you to Dawson."

"Like hell you are. I already have enough bodies behind me without adding you to the pile. I think we would all do well if the scientists attended to their studies and the Mounties attended to their duties."

"You don't have any choice. We both know that you need help. I may not be much, but at least you don't have to convince me of what's happening, and you know you can trust me."

"I'm coming too," Catherine said from the doorway, leaning against the doorframe. Richard looked over and saw his friend and recent comrade-in-arms. And he realized that this journey wasn't changing only him.

"I didn't want to speak for you, but I had a feeling you would say that, Catherine," Duran said.

"God, not another one," Richard said. "If Dawson turns out to be the carnage that I think it will be, you won't want your unborn child anywhere near there. You are in no condition to continue the trek. You are going to stay here at the observatory with Duran and Bouchard.

"I should think not," Catherine said. "My mind is made up."

Duran turned a concerned gaze to Catherine. "I have to agree with the Inspector on this. You look better than you did when you arrived, but you are certainly not up for travel."

"You'll only get in my way if you come," Richard said.

She rolled her eyes. "Yes, because I was such a liability back there on the trail when I saved both of our lives."

"Damn it, I still lead our party, and you are still a part of what's left of it, Catherine. You will obey my orders. You will stay here at the observatory until I can arrange for a safe escort back to Fort MacCammon."

Richard chewed his lip. His original plan was to arrive in Dawson and seize Morgan with a posse. Now, they were all dead, and Duran had asked good questions. He did not know who in Dawson could aid him, or who there he could trust.

"All right, then," Richard said. "You can come, Duran, and I thank you for your help. Catherine will stay here." He shot her a look before she could reply. "And that's the final word on the matter, Catherine."

Chapter 14

The next day, Richard left the observatory after eating a meal of tinned meat and beans. While he ate, Bouchard filled his pack with a generous amount of food and equipment. He laid a rifle next to Richard's pack, another lever-action Winchester, not unlike the one he owned. Richard gladly accepted, as it meant he didn't have to salvage supplies from the corpses still lying outside. He needed to make up for lost time if he were to make it to Dawson before the gold heist. Still, he had expected a three-day journey, and the trip was now on its fifth day. He thanked them and swore he would repay them twofold.

Newly outfitted, he was ready for the trudge towards Dawson. All that was left was for Catherine to wish him luck and kiss his cheek. Then, he and Duran departed.

Resting at the observatory had restored his muscles and tendons. Richard's leg muscles fired like pistons. With the wind at his back, and the path ahead already broken for them, the two men were making good time. Richard knew that he wasn't out of the woods (literally or figuratively). There was still a long distance between them and Dawson City, and they did not have the advantage of dogsleds to help with the journey.

A rustle in the trees followed by a flap of wings told him that there was still some life in the woods around them, just not much of the human kind. A gust of wind swirled snow into Richard's face. The few snowflakes that had started falling minutes ago had already increased into a flurry. Richard looked up and saw that the sky was cluttering with clouds. And he wondered if it were finally here, the great storm that he had felt circling above him these last few days. He had been waiting for it to descend on him.

"There's a bad storm about to hit us, Duran. We better pick up the pace."

As they passed the corpses of Azarov and his men, Richard tried to keep his eyes steady on the trail and clear to his objective. But he couldn't help but glance over to Lang. The dead Mountie's skin had become as pale as the surrounding snow. A heavy pile had blown over onto Lang, covering most of his face. Richard's disappointment in seeing a Mountie join with Morgan turned into anger. Richard never wanted to hurt anyone, but if there was any violence that he could live with, it was killing Lang. Azarov and the rest of his party may have been scum, but at least they never played at being anything better than that. But Lang had sworn an oath to uphold the law. For him, the Mountie uniform was nothing more than a disguise worn to trick and abuse the people he was supposed to protect. In that way, Lang was as bad as any swindler that ever stepped into the Yukon during the Gold Rush.

Duran, in contrast, couldn't stop the macabre need to look at the dead. Their limbs were frozen in place. Their eyeballs already snowed over. Their final expressions would stay locked until the spring, unless the scavengers came and removed them. Duran couldn't bear stepping over any of them. Instead, he tread around those horrifying statues with his wool hat removed as a gesture of respect.

"Do you want to have a moment of silence or say a few words, Inspector?" Duran asked.

Richard didn't bother to look at Duran when he said, "These men have nothing but silence now. And saying some words won't help them. Nobody in heaven would be listening."

They had only travelled for twenty minutes when Duran spoke up. "I want you to know that I appreciate your heroism, Inspector. I truly do. And I appreciate that you kept Bouchard and I out of the fight up until now. But I ask that you don't try anything as valiant as that again. I'm a part of this too now. Please don't try to exclude me."

"I promise," Richard said. He never had any intention of putting Duran in harm's way. But he needed help, and he had already decided on how to use Duran in the best way, though he wouldn't share it with Duran until the time came. Duran had already shown his defiant personality. Richard had no interest in listening to Duran challenge him every step of the way to Dawson. Rest assured, however, once they reached Dawson, Richard would place Duran somewhere safe. No one else would die under his leadership.

"Inspector, I have another matter to raise. Once we reach the trail, what about Constable Townsend, I mean, Mike? Will we give him a proper burial?"

"If he were on the way to Dawson, most certainly, but we don't have time for that. By the time we get off this path and onto the main trail, then head back to where we left him, we would be too late."

Richard kept it hidden, but his decision to leave Mike hurt him. He thought of Mike lying out there, surrounded by the paw prints of creatures who had fed upon him. Knowing that scavengers had likely picked at him, Richard couldn't bring himself to imagine what was now left of Mike's face. Mike never passed up a chance to chide Richard, and the chiding stung every time. But Mike was still a brother Mountie, and during some of the worst parts of Richard's life, he had been a companion.

Richard saw the glum expression on Duran's face.

"Have a heart, man," Richard said. "The worst is done. Surely, the nastiest parts are behind us."

Chapter 15

The storm that Richard had feared finally came. It was only due to their speed and Richard's trailman experience that the two men were saved from becoming lost. Visibility had become so bad that Duran suggested that they turn back while there was still time. Meanwhile, Richard watched as small cyclones of snow chalked over the black forest. The last of the tracks from Azarov's party, which he had been using as guideposts to Dawson, were quickly vanishing. Thus, the pair pressed on with a greater urgency. By the time they reached Dawson, the blizzard was at its height.

It was now six in the evening on their second day of travel from the observatory. At Dawson's entrance, the smells of chimney smoke and hot, buttered bread greeted them. As stormy as it was, the tired men were compelled to stop at the city's signpost.

"Let's rest here," Richard said.

His teeth were now beginning to chatter. They dropped their packs from weary shoulders and heaved themselves against a snowbank. Richard surveyed Dawson's streetscape. Dawson wasn't what it had been in the days of the Gold Rush, but between the fur trade and small-scale mining it was still lively enough to keep a scoundrel like Morgan in business.

There wasn't a single brick building in sight, but Richard saw telephone poles and buildings with carpentry as neat as would be found in a cathedral. He noticed that two new dressmaking shops, two jewellers, and a large grocery store had opened since his last visit. There was also a new barber shop standing where a vacant lot had been. A horse corral had been replaced with a laundry. Towering above them all was an office-storehouse owned by the Hudson's Bay Company. It reminded him of the company's presence throughout the north.

Electricity was coursing through the buildings. Through drawn curtains, Richard could make out silhouettes of people sitting down to supper — enjoying that hot, buttered bread.

"I see what I think is a coffeehouse down the street. Let's get ourselves warmed up before we make our next move." Duran said.

Richard nodded. They picked themselves up and followed a planked sidewalk past a photograph studio. He glanced at the framed pictures in the window, more reminders of progress. Dawson had blossomed into a sprawling metropolis of thirty thousand. The modernity around him was a relief from the forest that lingered in the back of Richard's mind.

"Hey, look over there," Duran said.

Richard looked across the street and saw an Anglican church — St. Paul's.

"That's where the slain reverend delivered his sermons," Richard said.

The snow obscured the church's front, but the two men could still see a sign posted there: MANY THANKS TO MR. ERIC MORGAN FOR HIS GENEROUS DONATION THAT MADE THE NEW STAINED-GLASS WINDOWS POSSIBLE. GOD BLESS YOU!

"I wonder if the donation was only to win favour with the church," Duran said.

"One thing is for certain: He didn't do it out of Christian spirit."

The pair walked into the coffeehouse. In spite of the storm, the place was crowded with people enjoying the last of their freedom before the blizzard left them all housebound for days. They stared at Richard and Duran while the two ordered bowls of hot soup and some coffee. It wasn't because they were unshaven or smelling of the woods. In Dawson, people were accustomed to seeing others who lived rough. But Richard and Duran were still a spectacle. The two men were exhausted but restless. Drained but still fidgeting with anxiety. An unspoken understanding ran through the room. These two strangers had a purpose. They were desperate for something yet unseen. No one spoke to them. They only continued their quiet conversations, likely hoping the pair would go away.

"Something tells me that the other customers don't want us here. We're lowering the mood of this place."

Richard huffed. "Well, all of these lords and ladies will have to excuse us. We didn't know we were attending the King's court when we walked through the door."

"So, how do we find Morgan?" Duran whispered.

"My God, Duran. He isn't in hiding. If he has this town under his thumb, as we believe he does, then he's running the largest gambling hall around. That's a good place to start. I'm almost certain that he'll be there overseeing his business."

A waitress delivered their soup.

"Excuse me, miss. Could you tell us where we can find the biggest gambling hall in Dawson?"

"Oh, that would be Eric Morgan's place," she said, pointing. "It's on Front Street."

Duran shot Richard a look, and Richard smiled.

"That was even easier than I thought it would be," Richard said and sipped his soup.

They ate in silence, and, as soon as they finished, Duran asked the question that Richard knew was coming.

"Along the trail, did you have time to craft a sensible plan, Inspector?" Duran said.

"Yes, I did. The way I see it, we can't rely on others for help in arresting Morgan. You were right about that. Instead, we'll arrest Morgan in front of as many people as possible. Arrested in plain sight, it will be impossible for Morgan or his cronies to make a move against us. Once we get the news of what happened on the trail to the town's telegraph station, it will relay the news to the outside world. In a day, everyone from Vancouver to Vienna will know of the attacks and the fallen heroes. The story will be too big for Morgan to conceal. Most of his supporters, lawmen or otherwise, will abandon him once that pressure is applied."

"Do you really believe that's the best approach?"

Richard leaned over the table. "It has to be this way, Duran. A man as powerful as Morgan can't be beaten only with brute strength. We need to strip away his power by exposing him to the world. Then the people in Dawson will see how small their bandit-king has become."

"That's where you come into the picture." Richard continued. "Duran, I need you to go over to the telegraph office. Inform the operator of what has happened and send word immediately to the RNWMP detachment at Fort McPherson in the Northwest Territories. We can trust them. Morgan's reach can't extend that far."

Duran cocked an eyebrow. "And can we trust the telegrapher?"

"If you suspect he's in Morgan's pocket, or if he tells you he's occupied with other work, give him this and tell him to handle your message immediately."

Richard removed his wedding band and handed it to Duran.

"While you're at it, you tell the telegrapher that Morgan is finished in the Yukon, and whatever his association is with this man up to today, the telegrapher had better get on the side of the angels right now."

Duran cocked an eyebrow. "Promise me again that you won't try to take Morgan alone. He'll have too much protection. Please, Inspector."

Richard saw the pleading in Duran's eyes.

"I promise," he said, and he wanted to mean it. "And you promise me that you won't hesitate to use that thing," Richard said while pointing at the shotgun over Duran's shoulder. "While you're at the station, I'll ask around for more details on Morgan and his operations. I'll start with the fine patrons of this place."

Duran agreed, took a last gulp of coffee, and rose from his seat. He patted Richard's shoulder and wished him luck. And as soon as he was through the door and out of sight, Richard walked out of the coffeehouse.

Chapter 16

As he saw it, Richard had killed two birds with one stone by sending Duran to the telegraph office. Word about Morgan truly needed to reach past the Yukon, but now Duran was also out of harm's way. Richard couldn't risk another life, and a citizen's life at that.

He headed for the gambling hall on Front Street. Men never became as successful as Morgan without working round-the-clock and keeping a close eye on their enterprises. Richard knew Morgan would be there to oversee his business.

At least sixty people had crowded into the hall. Richard moved past the oak roulette wheel. Its operator and six men were focused on its bouncing ball. No one noticed him, except for a red-haired girl. She gave Richard a cursory glance and apparently decided he wasn't a potential customer.

Reaching the bar, Richard shouldered between two bearded men in broad-brimmed, miner's hats. He leaned over the polished bar top.

"Bartender," he called.

The bartender was only five feet away, but he never looked at Richard. Instead, he explained the oil painting that hung behind the bar to three other customers. Richard gritted his teeth. Half of the enormous picture was covered by small kegs, so the painting hardly mattered.

"Bartender! Hey!"

"Yeah, what can I get you?"

"I'm Inspector Richard Carol with the Royal North West Mounted Police. I want Morgan."

The bartender straightened his back, and for the first time, made eye contact with Richard.

The bartender pointed to a man standing near a staircase. The pack of men and women flanking him were captivated by his small talk. He smiled at one lady and said something that must have been a compliment. She giggled, and this made him smile more.

Morgan looked younger than Richard imagined. The expectation was that years of playing Dawson's crime lord would have given Morgan deep facial lines and grey hair. This man looked only a few years older than Richard. His eyes smiled. His skin shone. Playful black hair poked from underneath a bowler hat. The tailored tweed suit looked like it cost two months of a Mountie's wages. Morgan's tie had a heavy pattern, which to Richard suggested that the man had a sense of humour. His belly rounded out the front of his shirt and coat. Morgan was a man who indulged in all of life's pleasures.

Richard stepped towards Morgan. The moment had come for the both of them. He stopped breathing. Two more steps and Richard would overtake his man.

He stood in front of Morgan, and Richard raised his hands, showing his badge and handcuffs. He said, "Eric Morgan, I'm Inspector Richard Carol of the North West Mounted Police. You've murdered a lot of people over the last few days. More than you could know. Your time is up. I'm placing you under arrest."

Smiling and shaking his head, Morgan's response looked so genuine, Richard could almost believe the man didn't know what the hell he was talking about.

"Murder," he said. "There must be some mistake, Inspector Carol. I've no cause to harm anyone. Any of my friends here will tell you that."

"They're going to need to find a new friend," Richard said. "You're going to hang for all that you've done. By God, I'll see to that. If you think Azarov and his men are going to save you, then you should know that they are already lying dead between here and Fort MacCammon."

Morgan's face changed then, and Richard knew that wasn't all that was changing. He drew half a breath and waited for the next move.

"It's a shame that you haven't brought along some friends of your own, Inspector," Morgan said.

He straightened and sauntered forward. His even tone unsettled Richard. Men accused of murder weren't supposed to be calm. For a wild second, Richard questioned whether the whole situation were only a dream. Any moment, he would awake in his bed at Fort MacCammon. Walter, Trapper, and everyone else would still be alive and ready for another day of police work.

"All right!" Morgan yelled. "Can I have your attention, everyone. The hall is closed. Everyone out now. Guests, workers, everyone, out!"

There were no protests or questions. The crowd made its way to the door with scarcely a murmur. Some of them never bothered to gather their mitts or hats, as if they planned on re-entering the hall in a few moments. The message to Richard was clear: *This won't take very long.* It took only a minute for the room to clear. In its execution, Richard saw how poor his grand plan was. Hoping that a public arrest would garner him some protection had been foolish.

Now, only Richard and Morgan remained. At least, that was what Richard believed until a hand fell on his shoulder. Even under his fur coat, he could feel the strong grip. The hand's owner must be a dangerous man — dangerous enough that, when the room emptied, he knew it was his job to stay behind and do the killing. Richard heard a pistol's hammer being cocked behind him. Another hand unslung the rifle from Richard's shoulder.

Morgan swaggered over to a piano and took a glass of scotch from its top. He gulped it like he was playing cards. Richard studied Morgan's casualness and concluded that he was enjoying his position of power. He also saw a wedding band on Morgan's hand and wondered what sort of woman could marry a monster like him.

"You gutless coward," Richard growled. "Maybe you were a hard man once, but now you've gone soft. You need other men to do all of your fighting and dirty work for you."

Morgan smiled and said, "You must be joking, Inspector. Do you know how much this suit cost? I wouldn't soil it over the likes of you."

He replaced his smile with a frown and took a step towards Richard.

"Inspector, now that everyone has left, we can speak plainly. I can't believe Azarov is dead. He was my best man. The rest of those men with him, I couldn't give a tin shit about them. So, did you kill Azarov?"

"Overconfidence killed Azarov."

Morgan nodded, unsurprised by the answer.

"I knew that you were coming, Inspector. One of my men at Fort MacCammon got word to me by your fort's own telegraph. Four regular Mounties, two special constables, and a nurse, right? From what I heard, Reverend Corbett gave you the full story, his signed testimony, and some letters from the Alderman boys. Well, you won't be keeping those on you for very much longer."

Morgan gulped from the scotch. "You never should have gotten this far. I ordered my Mounties at Fort MacCammon to kill you, and anyone else with you, on the trail. Then, when Azarov didn't come back on time, I figured that he was finishing you off. I even thought about sticking a couple of watchmen at the city's entrance, but I stupidly let *someone* dissuade me."

Morgan glanced past Richard's shoulder, and Richard heard the gunman behind him shuffle his feet.

"So, who was it that sent you the telegraph?" Richard said.

Morgan smiled and threw up his arms. "Why not tell you? It hardly matters now if you know who it was when you're about to die. And, God knows, I would want to know if I were you. So, to hell with it. It was Francis Drummond."

Francis. One of the men for whom Richard had sweated and bled. This man whom Richard felt he owed and who was owed justice. He was the traitor. And worst of all, Richard knew he was not the only one.

"Who else do you have in your pocket? Tell me. Like you said, it doesn't matter now if I know."

"Robert Donovan, Theodore Haines, and Walter Sands were all working for me too."

Richard's heart dropped. There were so many. "Francis and Walter both died on the trail in an ambush laid by Vadim Azarov and his party. The two special constables, Trapper and Henry, died too," Richard said.

Morgan rolled his eyes and considered for a moment. "Perhaps Walter and Francis did mean to kill you on the trail after all, but they were caught in Azarov's trap before they had the chance."

Such an accusation against Mounties, even against men he now knew to be traitors, was too much.

"Never," Richard said. "Walter insisted that his wife accompany us to Dawson. He never would have gotten her to go along with murder."

Morgan smiled, "Yes, I almost forgot about her. She's in Dawson too?"

"She's not. She's safe now, far away, where you can't reach her."

"We'll see about that. Still, I wonder why he wanted to bring her here."

"She learned of you, and so Walter said she was in jeopardy if she stayed at the fort. Being one of your men, he knew that she was in danger. Another one of your bastards would have silenced her, wouldn't they?"

"Probably. Hopefully." Morgan threw back his head and howled. "To think, he knew the danger she was in better than his superior officer because he himself was rotten!"

"For what it's worth, I will die thinking that Walter and Francis had more character than you. They saw that your game was finished, and they travelled with me to Dawson to answer for their crimes."

Morgan grimaced at Richard's resolve, so Richard pressed his attack.

He said, "How the hell do you plan to get out of this mess now? At least fifty people just saw a Mountie accuse you of being complicit in multiple murders."

"Do you think I'm a fool, Inspector? If I can pay people to smuggle things to and from Dawson, why couldn't I pay them to smuggle me? I've already made arrangements with some close Mountie friends to see to my release if I'm taken into custody. After I'm taken into custody for questioning concerning your death, they'll have me released and I will disappear. Indeed, I already packed a set of bags. I can be out of Dawson in less than an hour."

Morgan took another belt from the glass of scotch and shrugged. "I always like to give my men the benefit of the doubt, but I did make some preparations in case Azarov failed me. Oh, and of course, I'll pay for the safe passage of my closest men, like the one standing behind you. I can't leave my new right-hand man behind, can I? I have big plans for new business in America, and I need him by my side."

Morgan gave a smile and nodded his reassurance to the gunman at Richard's rear. Richard wondered if that man was buying any of the lies that Morgan had just spilled.

"Now it's time we said goodbye, Inspector."

Richard knew he had to get eyes on the man behind him before that man took Morgan's words as a cue to put a bullet in the back of Richard's head. He turned around, hands still held high, holding his badge and handcuffs. Richard was close enough to smell the chewing tobacco on the man's breath.

The gunman never noticed that Richard's raised hands had positioned his elbows only inches away from the gunman's own face. There was no time to see the swift elbow strike to the left temple. It put the man on his rear. The following kick to the man's chin folded his head back on his neck, as if it were on a hinge.

Morgan saw his one chance and lunged for the pistol still hanging at Richard's waist. Richard saw it too late. He knew all about Mounties being shot with their own pistols. The standard-issue holsters were too large, loose, and their flaps were too easily opened. A lift of the flap and a quick tug was all Morgan needed to do and the Colt would be free of its holster.

At only one yard's distance, Morgan levelled the Colt at Richard and pulled the trigger. Nothing happened. Morgan had clearly expected the ear-splitting bang and muzzle flash. The puzzlement on Morgan's face would have been worth placing in the window of that photographer's store.

Richard was on top of Morgan before he could overcome his surprise. His left hand snatched the pistol and pushed it back into Morgan's face. Morgan howled and hit the floorboards. On his way down, Morgan knocked over a tray of glasses, and they shattered all around him. Richard wasn't surprised to see a shard of glass had suddenly grown out of Morgan's palm. It was dangerously close to the wrist, and he knew it must be sending waves of pain up Morgan's arm. Richard pointed the pistol at the ceiling and fired. Within the confines of the gambling house, the shot was deafening.

"You see? My revolver works just fine. When the hangman asks you what happened, you can tell him, 'Sir, did you know that some Mounties carry their six-shot revolvers with only five rounds loaded? When you cock the hammer, the empty chamber is always the next one to be put into firing position. It's a good precaution for lawmen who are issued lousy holsters.'"

Richard then pointed the gun downwards and blew out Morgan's knee. Morgan howled, and his eyes rolled back into his head. Then he became silent. Richard thought the man had passed out, but he was only catching his breath to bawl again. Amid his yowling, Morgan grabbed what had been his right knee and tried to cover the waterfall of blood.

Richard had his man. Both of them were still alive. The arrest was going better than Richard had expected. As if jinxing himself, another of Morgan's cronies stepped through the hall's doorway, gun already in hand.

Thank God this idiot showed up late, Richard thought. If the man had arrived a few seconds earlier, he would have caught Richard with his back turned. One shot from Richard struck the latecomer's chest. The man got off a shot of his own before hitting the floorboards. Pain bit into Richard's right side. He looked down and saw a wet hole in his coat. The man's bullet had torn through Richard's lower torso just above the right hip. It didn't look like it had hit anything vital, but it hurt as badly as it bled.

The man groaned on the floor, and, for the second time that week, Richard killed a man when he was already down. He placed two bullets through the man's eyes and saw the two blasted-out pits pool with blood.

He reached down and seized Morgan by his black hair. Morgan howled, and Richard dragged him towards the door. For the first time, he saw fear in Morgan's eyes.

Despite Richard holding a handful of his hair, pulling Morgan was difficult. He wasn't a small man, and he thrashed about, kicking with his remaining good leg. Richard wished he had shot Morgan in the arm instead. Then, he could walk him to the police headquarters.

Before staggering through the doorway, Richard turned and surveyed the hall.

"I would burn this place down if I wasn't afraid of torching all of Front Street with it. Why should a whole street burn down over your dirty little business, hey, Morgan?"

Even in the fresh air, Morgan smelled of booze. The planked sidewalks were lined with people. At first, Richard thought it was the gunshot that brought them. He now saw how they were staring at Morgan. He realized that news had already bolted around town. Dawson's bandit-king had finally been apprehended.

A boy pointed and jabbered to his mother, like he was telling her something she wasn't already seeing. To the boy's right, a photographer rushed to set up his camera before the opportunity was lost. The shoes hitting the sidewalks had become a crackle as more people arrived.

By now, Richard could feel his right leg getting warm and wet, as if he had urinated.

How much blood can you lose before you faint? his inner voice asked. *I can't pass out now!*

Morgan panted, and Richard saw that pain and exertion were wearing on his adversary as well.

"Just stop for a second," Morgan said. "It doesn't have to be this way. If you let me go, I'll make you rich. I swear I will. You can leave the Mounties. Buy a huge house some place hot. Just let me go, and it's all yours!"

"I don't want your money. Keep it. You'll need every penny for your lawyer."

"If you don't want money, then what do you want? I could use a man like you in Dawson. Hell, I'll make you the top Mountie in the Yukon."

"Just what the north needs. Another Mountie under your thumb. I'll eat my own damn uniform before I wear it for you."

Morgan kept struggling, which frustrated Richard more with each step. He finally stopped, holstered his weapon and began pummeling Morgan. To the crowd, the scene was primal. Thrashing. Tearing. Screaming. A wild beast had fallen upon a weaker one. The onlookers winced when they heard the smacking of fist on face. That wet sound continued for too long. Shock, and a lack of sympathy for Morgan, held the people in place. The smacking went on.

Richard stopped punching when his hand could no longer make a fist. Morgan's face was long past recognizable. He wasn't moving any longer. Richard wondered if he had killed the man, and the worst part of him answered, *So what if you did?*

"Are you a Mountie?" one bystander asked.

"I'm Inspector Richard Carol of the Royal North West Mounted Police. I'm making an arrest," Richard said and wiped the blood from his swelling hand.

"What are the charges?" the man asked.

"What are you? His damned lawyer? When this dung maggot gains his senses, I'll give him the charges, which includes everything in the book up to murder."

He then removed his handcuffs and placed them on Morgan. Never had snapping them closed given Richard such relief.

Chapter 17

By the time Richard reached the headquarters' courtyard, four hundred yards from the gambling hall, most of the Mounties in town had already assembled there. Uncharacteristically, they did not act. They watched in disbelief and murmured to one another. The exceptions were the few who had been ordered to move behind Richard. Whether they did so to keep back the wave of citizens to his rear, or to keep him from escaping, he was unsure.

The detachment's senior commander, the superintendent, stepped forward.

"Inspector! Who is that man at your feet? What in the devil have you gotten this city into, man?"

Richard had to yell over the storm so everyone would hear. "You know damned well who I'm holding, and you know damn well why I'm holding him!"

"You have no right to handle that man so!"

"The three murdered Mounties and two special constables that I left back on the trail give me the right."

There was nothing at first. Then, underneath the wind, Richard heard the chatter among the Mounties. Some had doubts. Some were confused. Some thought that they had misheard him.

"No, my good men," Richard said in a louder voice. "You all heard me correctly. Our brothers are dead. They were attacked by surprise while in the performance of their sworn duties. With no time to act or react, it could have been any one of you who died at the hands of thieves and cowards."

He was about to mention the day's now foiled gold heist, but thought better of it. All the Mounties who were accomplices would have figured out by now that the robbery was cancelled. And those who were innocent already had enough shock to contend with. More outlandish news might drive them deeper into disbelief. He had to persuade them, not astonish them.

"Don't you all see? Morgan's power lies in his ability to contain knowledge of his crimes to Dawson. It lets him run this place as his own little kingdom. But, I've already sent a man to give word of the murders, and all that has happened to Fort McPherson. By now, my man would have already visited Dawson's telegraph office and sent word. By tomorrow, that word will have spread across the British Empire. Morgan has now been exposed to the world. It's over, gentlemen. He's over."

"I know that there are men here who have been party to this man's enterprise. And I know that some men may not have participated, but had knowledge of it all. Whatever the future holds for these men, that is for the court to decide, and each one will have to live with his own conscience after that. What I'm asking for today is that justice be served and duty done. I need all of you to step forward, for the Royal North West Mounted Police, and join me in tearing down the ungodly architecture that Morgan has built."

Dizziness overtook him suddenly, and Richard collapsed to one knee. His hand went to his wounded side. He had lost so much blood. He looked at the band of Mounties before him and tried to see himself through their eyes. Bloody, weak, and doubtful.

None of them moved. He was sure he had left them uninspired. He waited for the handcuffs or the bullet to the back of the head. Then, one Mountie stepped forward. Without looking at Richard, he snapped his boot heel to the ground and said, "I'm with you, sir."

Before Richard could respond, a second Mountie stepped forward. With his head held high, he said, "Ready to serve, Inspector."

A third Mountie came. More followed. In short time, every Mountie present had moved towards Richard. They had made their choice. Some looked more reluctant than others. Richard wondered if these were the ones who had been Morgan's accomplices. *No matter now*, he thought. Today, they were all on his side. He heard calls from behind him.

One elderly woman, who had braved the blizzard to come see the spectacle, yelled, "We are with you too!"

Another woman called, "We'll stand with you!"

A chorus of cheers filled the air and overwhelmed the storm. Richard looked back at Dawson's citizens and saw that a crowd of hundreds was taking small steps forward. He whispered, "Thank you." He had never been so grateful.

A groan rose from the ground. Richard looked down and saw Morgan staring at him. "Take a good look before your eyes swell shut, maggot. Take a good look and see that the Mounties are with me. The townspeople are with me. Dawson is with me. It's the Royal North West Mounted Police and Dawson City that have won this day."

Epilogue

He stared through the glass pane. An April shower obscured the view, but Richard could still make out the figures. Two of them were carrying firewood to their home. He figured that they would need it tonight. It was cold now, and, in a few hours, nightfall would bring even more bitter temperatures. Richard felt a draft blowing along the window frame. He wished he was sitting closer to the hotel's fireplace. However, the Brownstone was crowded that day. A group of land surveyors were passing through Fort MacCammon, and they had taken up most of the hotel's tables.

"Here's your food, Inspector," Melissa said. She placed before him a steaming pile of moose meat and roasted potatoes slathered in gravy.

She smiled at him, but her smile had changed since the events four months earlier. It was now spiced with admiration. Everyone at Fort MacCammon was treating him differently now. The avoidance that he had felt from the other Mounties had melted away. They had gained a new respect for a man who was becoming a legend in northern Canada. And the missionaries at the church came to him at least once a week to discuss their plans and activities. *They* came to him. So much had changed in the last few months.

As Richard expected, news of the tragedy had travelled fast over the telegraph lines. And it did shake the British Empire. Ambushes in the wilderness? Dead Mounties? A crime lord in the Arctic? Every newsman in the world saw the potential for headlines.

The scandal and investigation led some people to consider disbanding the RNWMP's Dawson City detachment. Sensible people never saw that as a real choice. Instead, most of the Mounties who served there were redeployed elsewhere and replaced. For the RNWMP, it was bound to become another part of the service's folklore.

Senior officers had been dispatched to investigate. During his meetings with them, Richard had been asked several times if he was ever asked to join with Morgan. He thought of Morgan's offer at the gambling hall, but said nothing.

Morgan had avoided the hangman's noose. The evidence against him was undeniable, but he gave up the other members of his gang in exchange for leniency. A total of seventy of his men and women were offered up in this deal. People who worked at the post office, the docks, the telegraph office, all went down with Morgan, including eight Mounties. Richard took some comfort in knowing that Morgan would die before he ever breathed free air again.

Richard thought of Francis and Walter, and how the two had betrayed the service. He thought that perhaps it was for the best that the pair had died in that ambush. If they had survived, what then? Would they have tried to kill him? Could he say for certain that they wouldn't have? And if they did try, would he have had any other recourse than to kill them while defending himself?

He scooped a heap of mashed potatoes into his mouth and tried to shake off these ill thoughts, but they persisted. Most distressing for Richard was Catherine's fate. As he had feared, she was now an outcast. The Mounties had questioned her about her involvement and knowledge in Morgan's dealings, and she repeatedly pleaded her innocence. Still, the stain of having a corrupt Mountie as a husband would not wash away. Richard hadn't seen her since they parted at the observatory. She had been staying with family in Dawson. Richard imagined that she was packing her bags to leave the Yukon. It would be what he would do in her place.

He cut through the moose and rubbed it into the gravy. He heard the door open and looked towards the Brownstone's entrance. There she was. Catherine. She smiled when she saw him, clearly unsurprised to find him there. In her arms, she held a bundle of fur. Through a hole in the top, Richard saw two eyes shining outwards.

"Catherine, I was just thinking about you, and suddenly you're here!" he said as he stood and went to her.

Richard wrapped his arms around her and she buried her face against his neck. The surveyors couldn't help but watch this show. When they separated, Richard could see that her eyes were wet.

He pulled out a chair for her and they took their seats. He reached over and brushed the baby's cheeks, which were full of colour. The baby cooed when Richard touched him.

"He's not shy of strangers, is he?" Richard said and got a giggle from Catherine. "When did you get back to the fort?"

"This morning. The trip here was nowhere near as bad as I thought it was going to be, what with this little one and all. I swear, it seemed like he slept most of the way here."

"I was so glad to hear that the baby made it through all right," Richard said. "It was a shock to me when I learned that you named him *Richard*."

"I know what you're thinking. Why didn't I name him after Walter? The truth is, I loved Walter, but you were the one who saved my baby. You'll always have a special place in both of our hearts for that."

Her words made Richard's own heart miss a beat. Little Richard wiggled his head out of his fur blanket.

"Hey, look, he must know that we're talking about him," Richard said. "It's such a surprise to see you two. You look well, Catherine."

"Thank you, but it hasn't been easy for me."

"If there is anything that anyone can do, please come to me first."

"I will. Thank you, Richard. For everything. I'm not so certain I'm the same woman I was when we started all of this."

"I don't think either of us are the same," he said. "What are your plans for the future?"

She frowned at him. "I think you already know that I can't stay here, Richard. No one in the Yukon wants to look at the wife of one of the corrupt Mounties. I've been offered a job at a hospital in Montreal."

"Better start practising your French."

She laughed, and it raised Richard's spirits to see that she could still smile. She reached across the table and took his hand.

"How are your wounds healing?" she said.

Richard chuckled.

"They're hardly worth mentioning. They looked worse than they were," he lied. "And if anything, they enhanced my reputation among the officers and men."

"Oh?"

"Wounded Mounties are always given an added measure of respect, my dear."

Catherine signalled the waitress for a cup of coffee.

"Yes, I know all about it. I read your name in the newspaper more than once, and I've heard that the grateful people of Dawson gave you a bag of gold."

Richard shrugged. "They were grateful, and it isn't as if it's the first time Dawson gave a Mountie a well-deserved award. You know, when Sam Steele left Dawson, they gave him more gold than me, and I took a bullet for that town. Besides, how could I turn it down? It was the reverend's widow herself who proposed it."

"I'm not judging," she said, and raised her hands in mock defence. "And if you've taken a drink now and then to help you get through all of this, I wouldn't blame you for that either."

"I haven't. It certainly isn't what my mind needs just now."

"I'm so glad to hear it," she said. Melissa delivered fresh coffee. She gave the baby a smile as she placed the cup down far away from the baby.

Catherine sipped from the cup and recoiled when she found it too hot. "I suspect that you must wonder if I knew about Walter."

Her cautious eyes told him that she had been waiting to hear his opinion on this for a long time."

"No, I never thought you knew," Richard said. "Why would Walter put you at risk by telling you? Some may question his integrity as a Mountie, but he was a man who loved you and wanted to protect you. I've no doubt about that."

He squeezed her hand as a sign of sincerity. Her eyes welled and a tear rolled down the corner of one. Richard wished that he would one day learn to shorten his statements by a sentence or two.

"I feel like such a fool," she said. "I never asked where the new money was coming from. Years ago, Walter told me that he inherited some money from an uncle, so I assumed that was it."

"Anyway, what about you? What's your plan for when you return to Toronto?"

"I'm not leaving," Richard replied.

"What? You want to stay in the Yukon? I'm surprised, Richard. I would think that this would be your chance to leave the north. Doesn't the south hold more opportunities for advancement up the ranks? Why, the Hero of Dawson City could go anywhere in Canada. You know that you're a shoe-in for lecturing. How many other policemen and explorers returned to the south's big cities as guest presenters at the universities? The schools in Toronto, Montreal, and New York can't get enough of the Arctic these days."

Richard knew what she said was true. Chances for promotion in the RNWMP were slim, and what few there were lay in the south. As for academia, the north was a new frontier to be researched and examined: botany, zoology, anthropology, meteorology … there were never-ending veins of knowledge to be mined as much as the Yukon was during the Gold Rush. Men like Richard were a main conduit of knowledge between the Arctic and scholars.

"Sure, there's plenty of opportunity with the academics, but the Yukon still has much to offer." Richard leaned forward and squeezed her hand again. "You see, the Yukon was never the problem for me. I was. I can see that now. There are great prospects for a Mountie who has the right attitude. The police service in the north is still being reshaped. New rules and practices will be applied. New members will need to be brought up to speed. New relations with the citizens will have to be built."

"Well, I'm sure you'll find your rightful place in the new order."

"I know I will. The Royal North West Mounted Police is changing the Yukon and changing *in* the Yukon. I want to be here for that. I want to be a part of that."

Author's Note

Though this novel is fictitious, it closely aligns with actual events that transpired in the late nineteenth and early twentieth centuries. The Mounties actually conducted winter patrols between places like Fort McPherson (NWT) and Dawson City (Yukon). These patrols were filled with danger, as demonstrated in 1911 when one patrol became lost on the trail and all four Mounties died.

The biggest break from historical fact (apart from the characters) is Fort MacCammon and the Little Fox River on which it sits. They were created only to control for the time and geography that I needed to tell the story.

Several times the book refers to the aboriginal people of the region. By these, I mean the people who can trace their full (or a significant part of their) ancestry to groups that have, according to the earliest records, existed in Canada before all others. I sincerely hope that I have reflected their culture and history with all due respect.

Lastly, I want to be clear that the corruption among members of the Royal North West Mounted Police is completely fictional. In all my research, I never found any instances of them robbing gold shipments (though they guarded plenty) or participating in a criminal organization in Dawson City. By all accounts, the Mounties conducted themselves honestly and with the admiration of the Yukon's citizens.

Acknowledgements

So many people have helped me to write this book, but special gratitude goes to my wife, Carolyn. She always gave me excellent advice, helping me to shape ideas and clarify thoughts. Thank you, baby!

CPSIA information can be obtained
at www.ICGtesting.com
Printed in the USA
LVHW040305131218
600305LV00001B/232/P

9 781771 802222